Wisdom's Way

Wisdom's Way

101 Tales of Chinese Wit

Translated & Enhanced by Walton C. Lee

YMAA Publication Center
Jamaica Plain, Mass. USA

YMAA Publication Center
38 Hyde Park Avenue
Jamaica Plain, Massachusetts, 02130

ISBN:1-886969-36-1

Printed in Canada

3

Publisher's Cataloging in Publication
(Prepared by Quality Books Inc.)

Feng, Meng-lung, 1574-1646.
   [Chih nang. English]
   Wisdom's way : 101 tales of Chinese wit / compiled and
translated by Walton Lee.
   p. cm.
   ISBN: 1-886969-36-1

   1. Anecdotes—China. 2. Wisdom. I. Lee, Walton. II. Title.
II. Title.

PN6267.C5F46 1997   895.1'46
                                            QBI97-40077

Editor's Note:
   Due to the unfortunate disunity among romanization systems,
Mr. Lee devised the translation and spelling of all posthumous titles
and epithets of the emperors and lords, as well as all the Chinese
names. Names refered to in the text may be found in written
Chinese in the endnote section of the book.

Dedication

This book is dedicated to my nieces and nephews:
Tina, Anthony, William, and Irene

Acknowledgments

I am grateful to Mr. Edwin B. Massey for his correction of my grammar; to Mr. Andrew Murray for his preparation of the manuscript; to Mr. Tim Comrie for typesetting; to Ms. Deborah Clark for the cover design; to Mr. David Lepp for his illustrations; to Mr. Cheng Ku for his assistance with setting up the Web site; and to my brother, Mr. Stephen C. Lee, for taking my photo for this book.

Contents

Preface

An emperor once remarked: "History is a mirror. Studying it mindfully, you will learn the causes of a dynasty's growth, decline, and fall." In ancient China, as a tradition, every emperor had two personal historians. One was meticulously writing down His Majesty's conversations and the other his behavior. Unfortunately most of these detailed records were destroyed between dynasties, in wars and riots. However, every dynasty had at least one set of official history made by its successor. After overthrowing an old empire and taking over all the royal documents, the new emperor, or his offspring, would often appoint historians to edit and publish those documents in biographical form.

Twenty-six sets of these histories have survived. Covering over 2,500 years, there are more than three hundred volumes, each one averaging 250 to 300 pages in length. Reading this collection was and is a favorite pastime of Chinese intellectuals, who find it significant for both its historical and literary content.

One such reader was Feng, Mon-Lon (1574-1646 A.D.). Feng worked as a low-level clerk in the imperial service for most of his life. Politically, he had no hope for advancement. Living at the end of the Ming dynasty (1368 A.D. to 1644 A.D.), he was a frequent eye-witness to government corruption. He clearly foresaw the decline and eventual collapse of the huge Ming empire. Though perceiving this unavoidable destruction, as a low-level official Feng was miserably powerless.

Powerless, but not without hope. In 1626 he began copying from what was then only twenty four sets of official history and from other books. In only two months, he collected over 1,200 anecdotes and categorized them according to levels of wisdom. Feng's objective was to lecture the educated to be broad-minded and far-sighted, otherwise catastrophe would soon visit them. His ominous prediction became true. The decaying Ming dynasty was overthrown seventeen years later.

Wisdom's Way is an offspring of Feng, Mon-Lon's extensive collection of anecdotes. In its 101 stories, some true, some passed down from legend and popular lore, you will find many clues to the culture of China, and to human nature and interpersonal relationships.

To set the scene for these stories, you should understand an element of Chinese culture. In the old days, there were four classes in China: the educated, the farmers, the laborers, and the merchants. Each one of them had to follow a strict set of moral rules and a rigid code of social conduct.

For example, success in politics was the goal of the educated. It brought prestige to the individual and his family. Education was the only way to achieve this goal. Only by passing three extremely competitive national examinations could a person generally receive political appointments — usually to small and remote cities. This was the bottom of the political hierarchy. From the small cities and outlying provinces, these educated appointees would laboriously work their way back to the central government in hopes of becoming high-ranking officials. Only a handful of the intelligentsia passed all three exams. The majority of the educated class would pass only one or two exams in their whole lifetime, and usually end up becoming private tutors or government clerks.

Feng's collection is treasured by Chinese intellectuals. Now, Western readers can enjoy these tales of sophisticated Chinese wisdom. I believe that Western readers will also be fascinated by the political intrigue and shrewd problem-solving skills demonstrated in these stories.

Because the original edition of Feng's collection was unavailable, I used the contemporary revised version. By translating and enhancing this collection from dry and rigid classical Chinese to simple and colorful English, I hope to engage a new generation of both Chinese and Western readers.

Walton C. Lee
El Cerrito, CA

PART ONE

Supreme Wisdom

There is no single rule of wisdom. What matters is how you use it. Consequently, even a blockhead sometimes makes a smart choice, or a genius makes a foolish one. Why? The Supreme Wisdom naturally flows from one's mind and answers the problem; there is no need to rack one's brain for a solution. The wise person positions him or herself outside of a problem and analyzes it, always looking at the puzzle from a larger perspective, before undertaking any solution. He or she weighs the ultimate long-term advantages against the immediate short-term disadvantages.

At the other end of the human spectrum, the narrow-minded person approaches problems with tunnel vision, confounded by immediate gain or short-term loss. While the wise person is calm and rational in a crisis, the impatient person is worried, emotional and irritated. These states of mind are counterproductive when dealing with a dilemma. Facing a problem, the person with Supreme Wisdom always behaves, in the beginning, ordinarily, and even indifferently. But the outcome is remarkable and even astounding to average people. It is a rare and unique talent to be capable of following the Supreme Wisdom, which can be divided into four categories. Here are several stories to illustrate my point.

CHAPTER ONE

Look at the Whole Picture

How to Rule a Country

Warring States Period
475 B.C. to 221 B.C.

This conversation occured in 312 B.C. during the Warring States period. China was unfortunately in disunity as a handful of kings and lords jockeyed for domination. The country of Yang had been devasted by a palace insurrection and an invasion, and the older ruler had suffered an untimely and humiliating death. After visiting the sacked city and wounded soldiers, the new king Yang-Jau[1] was disturbed, and wondered how a similar situation could be prevented.

"How should I manage my country?" he asked one of his advisors, a man named Guo Wai.[2]

"Your Majesty, if you want to be an Emperor," the advisor explained, "you should treat your subordinates as teachers. To be a King, you should treat them as friends. To be a Lord, you should treat them as guests. If you wish to ruin your country, if I may say, you should treat them as servants or even slaves. The choice is yours alone."

Impressed and a little surprised, the king politely returned, "Your statement is very interesting. Since I desire to be an Emperor, whom should I begin to respect?"

"Your Majesty might start with me," the advisor boldly suggested, "a little-known person. As a result, other capable individuals, with greater reputations, will be envious and come to try their political fortunes here. These intellectuals, whose counsel you seek and esteem, having heard of your generosity and expecting to be treated likewise, will confidently approach Your Majesty and freely present their ideas and suggestions. Your Majesty may then choose the best administers from among them. Thus our country's prosperity and

Your Majesty's potency is surely secured."

The king was well pleased and acted swiftly. Besides providing his advisor with an exceptionally generous salary, this smart ruler also ordered his royal architect to design and construct a splendid villa for him. This news rapidly spread among neighboring countries. Hearing this, people were amazed. Many well-educated gentlemen resigned their current positions and relocated themselves to this country. In less than three years, after meticulous selections and severe competitions, a handful of distinguished and competent foreigners were properly appointed, with similar generous treatment from the king. They helped him to efficiently manage his country and steadily expand its borders.

The advisor really understood one of humankind's most important abilities; utilize the wisdom of others to establish one's success.

The Right People
Spring and Autumn Period
770 B.C. to 476 B.C.

One day, Confucius's horse ran away and trampled a neighbor's rice field. The victimized farmer was infuriated and retained the vandalizing horse. Upon hearing of this misfortune, Confucius immediately instructed Tzy Gon,[3] one of his best students, to negotiate with the farmer, compensate him for the damage, and win the release of the animal. Tzy Gon arrived at this rural area, and after a few inquiries, this well-dressed student, in the polished language and manner of the upper-class, apologized to this illiterate farmer, and tried to settle the matter as two gentlemen would.

However, after a brief conversation, this farmer was baffled by the visitor's fine talk and hurriedly retreated home, hiding behind a tightly bolted door. Standing in the front yard, the student courteously explained his intention. Understanding none of the elegant words, the farmer, puzzled and irritated, stubbornly refused to receive him again. After a whole day of fruitless effort, the student, exhausted and frustrated, went back and reported his failure.

"You two are from totally different social levels," Confucius beamed a profound smile and calmly remarked. "Your attempt to reason with the farmer is like serving expensive and delicious dishes to a cow or playing beautifully composed music to a chicken. They couldn't appreciate or understand it at all."

Next morning, Confucius dispatched his horseman to handle the problem. After a brief dialogue, the farmer happily accepted the terms and returned the horse.

Different people have different abilities. Only a wise person can manage these differences appropriately. Because of their different backgrounds, the literate student's refined language wasn't understood by the uneducated farmer. Even if the student had used a coarse dialect, which might have been taken as a mockery, the farmer wouldn't have felt comfortable communicating with him.

Then why didn't Confucius send his horseman in the first place? Because he understood that his well-bred student, in his arrogance, would have felt offended if he, an educated and capable gentleman, was not sent. Confucius also saw that, after the student had failed his mission, the horseman's success would be valued all the more by the other students. The wise man perceived that his students and servants would profit equally from the experience.

A Drunken Bodyguard

Western Han Dynasty
206 B.C. to 25 A.D.

Once, a famous prime minister named Bin Jyi[4] was on his way to attend a party. One of his bodyguards was a little drunk, and suddenly threw up on the carpet of the carriage.

"How dare you?" an assistant promptly scolded, and then with great embarrassment and uneasiness, asked his master "Your Highness, should I discharge this lout on the spot?"

"Of course not," the prime minister responded tranquilly, not showing any anger at all. "Such a fine young man! If you discharged him, he, bearing such a disreputable stigma, couldn't find a proper job elsewhere. I don't want to ruin his future. Be considerate and kind to others. He only accidentally stained part of the carpet, which is not a terrible crime. I don't mind it at all."

In that era, life was cheap—especially the lives of servants and slaves. For similar trivial offenses, a servant often would be severely punished or even put to death. The assistant, at first baffled by his master's generosity, reluctantly conveyed this decree to the frightened bodyguard, who was amazed yet profoundly appreciative. After that incident, the prime minister unconsciously acquired an exceptionally loyal servant, who would willingly sacrifice his own life for his warm-hearted master.

The bodyguard, who was from the western border, once, on a leave of absence, returned to his native village. Overhearing a rumor that the nearby barbarians intended to invade the frontier, he immediately returned and delivered this piece of vitally important information to his master, who duly reinforced the garrisons there. Several days later, a war broke out. Since the army was pre-warned and well-prepared, the casualties were low and the attack unsuccessful.

Later, at an imperial military conference, the emperor quizzed all of his high-ranking officials and senior generals, one by one, about this invasion. Nobody could provide satisfactory background knowledge except the prime minister, who was highly praised. He was rewarded handsomely by the emperor.

Always strew the seeds of small kindness. Some of those seeds might cultivate and become flowers of success in the future.

Hire a Leading Gangster
Tang Dynasty
618 A.D. to 907 A.D.

One day in the late seventh century A.D., the emperor Tang-Kao "Magnificent"[5] wanted to visit a city located several hundred miles from the imperial palace. Due to famine and plague, many starving farmers had abandoned their lands and became ruthless highwaymen. They frequently held up and even killed travelers on unguarded routes. Nobody dared to leave the city without heavy protection. Some of the most notorious gangsters frequently raided the suburban areas of the capital city. The emperor was deeply worried for his safety, and dispatched a competent censor Wai Yuan-Jong,[6] as an advance unit, to secure the road.

Confidently accepting this tough task, the official, to all of his colleagues'

surprise, flatly declined an offer to receive a company of well-trained imperial soldiers as bodyguards, and abruptly called on a nearby prison. After a few
minutes of scrutiny, he hand-picked a notorious gangster, generously provided him with clean clothes and a delicious meal, and immediately hired him
as his bodyguard.

After several days of intense observation, the official confidently promoted this bodyguard to become the chief inspector for his advance unit. This
gangster was astonished by his unexpected good fortune and deeply appreciated the official for this new position. To prove his ability and repay his master's kindness, the gangster, with tens of years experience as a criminal, did his
best to assure the tranquillity of this imperial journey. With hundreds of fully-
loaded carriages and thousands of servants and eunuchs, the royal caravan
was a slow and wealthy target. But the emperor proceeded peacefully. Not a
penny was lost.

Everyone is useful on some occasions in some ways. With proper guid-
ance, a chimpanzee can communicate with people. On the other hand, in
the wrong time and place, a well-educated gentleman can become a shameless swindler or a dangerous murderer. People always appreciate opportunity
and recognition. Through observation, a wise person can properly motivate,
utilize and maximize other people's potential ability and attain a faithful and
dedicated servant.

An Encouraging Praise

Tang Dynasty
618 A.D. to 907 A.D.

A high-ranking government official named Leou Bei,[7] who was also a
well-known scholar in classical literature, was demoted to the position of
mayor and assigned to a remote and uncultivated region, where people lived
side by side with native residents. The natives' culture and living standards
were totally different and very primitive.

One day, a local chieftain's son, who had for years dedicated himself to
the study of literature, with only moderate success, humbly called on Leou
Bei and presented some of his finest works for comment. Carefully reading
each work, this new mayor was obviously pleased, and first highly praised

those mediocre articles and then gave some helpful suggestions. With deep appreciation, the visitor enthusiastically thanked the mayor and left.

One of the mayor's assistants, standing nearby, who viewed the works and knew the compliments were undeserved, curiously and politely asked "Sir, I am puzzled. If I may ask, why didn't you give your objective opinion of those third-rate works?"

"Please." The master was silent, pondering for a moment, and then calmly responded. "This is a less progressive area. We shouldn't use our well-polished literary yardstick to measure their performance. We should judge them according to their situation and by their own merits. That young man, whose father is an illiterate chieftain, has studied very hard without the benefit of a teacher, and showed courage to make an appointment with me to review his articles. I shouldn't let him down. After receiving my favorable comments, he will faithfully follow my recommendations. His peers will be impressed and follow him. I must encourage him to continue learning our culture, which will benefit both himself and our country. Education can eliminate ignorance, reduce mis-communication, and avoid future troubles. Consequently, it will diminish the degree of friction and conflict between newcomers and natives. In the long run, it will positively contribute to the tranquillity of our dynasty. Why should I be stingy and harshly critical when it costs me nothing to give a few well-deserved compliments?"

The mayor's assistant was deeply impressed with his master's insight.

Suggestions will be better accepted if preceded by general compliments instead of well-intentioned criticisms, which might irritate or dishearten the seeker.

Grab the Right Stocks

Chin Dynasty
221 B.C. to 206 B.C.

At the end of 206 B.C., the Chin dynasty was overthrown and the new order not yet established. While troops swarmed through the wrecked capital city, generals and officers were busy directing their soldiers to loot the grandiose imperial palace and the mansions of rich men. Every soldier laboriously carried gold or silver bullion, expensive jewelry, and precious antiques.

However, one far-sighted commissioner named Hsiao Ho[8] ordered his subordinates to take over the Bureau of Information. Instead of treasures, his soldiers hauled away many cartloads of military maps, social data, population charts, and important statistics.

Shortly after this devastating pillage, a bloody civil war broke out. Those recovered charts and maps displayed the importance of some strategic locations and revealed many concealed caches of weapons and stores. Hsiao Ho's master, King Han, was greatly pleased with this vital information, and highly praised this perceptive commissioner, who later became the first appointed prime minister. During the same chaotic period, while most people focused on hoarding precious metals, a clerk gathered quantities of wheat and flour. Soon came the destructive civil war. Farmers couldn't plant their wheat fields, and food prices skyrocketed. Grains became as valuable as gold. This clerk sold his stores bit by bit, and earned an immense profit. Others, holding gold bullion and jewelry, didn't know where to exchange their wealth for food and starved to death. Thousands of people perished.

From these two cases, we see that gold and valuables, which we ordinarily cherish, are not necessarily the most important possessions in a time of chaos. Only a person with farsightedness and wisdom can perceive a coming crisis and react accordingly.

I am Afraid of Something Else   *Warring States Period 475 B.C. to 221 B.C.*

In the Warring States period China was unfortunately divided into several politically independent regions, which frequently made war against one another. Between military conflicts, diplomats and politicians worked to make alliances and agreements. In those days, signing a well-drafted treaty was as important as winning a battle.

In a middle-sized country, a capable commissioner named Lin Shan-Lu,[9] due to his outstanding performance on a recent diplomatic mission, was unconventionally promoted to be a prime minister. Hearing this news, the minister of defense, an old veteran general, Lian Poo,[10] who had fought many battles over the last thirty years, was displeased with this quick advancement.

"Damn it! I've risked my life in battle for years to get where I am." the minister of defense often grumbled. "That cock-eyed upstart uses only his silver tongue and leaps over me! It's totally ridiculous. I must cut him down to size in public."

Hearing of this, the new prime minister deliberately avoided this bull-headed general. Rumors circulated that the new prime minister was cowardly and afraid to confront the old general. In a private party, some of his intimate assistants, with indignation, asked him about the reason.

"Gentlemen, allow me to clarify myself once for all," the prime minister calmly explained. "Could this general be in any way equal to the hot-tempered King Chin, a most powerful king and our western neighbor?"

The audience agreed that a general was certainly not equal to a king.

"Yet in our last conference," continued the prime minister, "I humiliated this rude and ill-intentioned king in front of several thousand of his well-armed bodyguards. In truth, I am afraid of no one. However, in our country, there are other factors I must take into account. Our belligerent western neighbor always wants to subdue us, but because of the general's ability and my wisdom, they dare not risk invading us. However, if the general and I quarrel among ourselves, our country's future for sure would be doomed. For this reason alone I yield, and will not confront this respectable and capable general. It is all for the tranquillity of our people and country, not my own reputation."

All of his listeners agreed and nodded their heads, deeply impressed with the prime minister's reasoning. Learning of this, the general felt remorseful for his inconsiderateness and short-sightedness. With shame and regret, he humbly visited this young prime minister and politely asked for forgiveness, which was promptly granted. After that incident, the two men cooperated closely with one another and eventually became best friends. During their lifetime, the western neighbor never had a chance to conquer this country.

In a turbulent period, especially for a small country situated between strong powers, an internal unity is essential—together they succeed, apart they fail. A competent person always has to consider all factors, not only his own reputation.

By Compliment

Sui Dynasty
581 A.D. to 618 A.D.

In the early seventh century A.D., China was unfortunately in disunity as the short-lived Sui dynasty was overthrown. Several lords and kings were competing for the throne. Civil war started. People were slaughtered like cattle. Cities were devastated. After a few days of brutal struggle and uncertainty, the lord Lee Yuan,[11] who would eventually become the emperor, finally won a decisive battle and occupied a strategically important city. Collecting all the booty and confiscating his opponents' valuables, he intended to distribute this booty to the soldiers and people. Some old-fashioned generals suggested, according to tradition, that he treat citizens and slaves differently.

"Why?" the lord flatly remarked. "The enemy's arrows and swords had no eyes and didn't favor either of the groups. Taking the same chance, they risked their necks for the victory and the reward. It's only fair that I treat them equally." He then gave out petty positions, with a salary that would support the recipients for the rest of their natural lives, to those persons who wanted to resign and return to their native villages and become farmers again.

This generous behavior was unheard of. All of the treasurers and accountants were astonished. They vigorously protested to him about this policy and its potentially huge costs for the national budget in the future.

"Don't be ridiculous! I want to be a emperor. How can I afford to be stingy? A penny-wise person will never build an empire," the lord declared confidently. "One of the former dynasty's biggest mistakes was its stinginess. The rich had accumulated tremendous wealth and didn't spare anything for the penniless, who rose up and defeated them. Be farsighted and look at the whole picture. I am only one of a handful of potential rulers. To secure my position I must win over the people, not with force and battles, but with money and positions. Politics is an art, not a science. It has nothing to do with accounting and balance sheets. Why should I not be generous?"

What Should I Purchase?

Warring States Period
475 B.C. to 221 B.C.

In the Warring States period, China was unfortunately divided into a handful of countries. They were frequently at war with one another. Civilians were slaughtered by the thousands. Competent people were always in great demand by the governments. Consequently, as a custom, wealthy princes and lords provided free lodging, food, and a regular salary to attract people with talents and abilities. They would be hired as political consultants or, if there were no vacancies, be called "house-guests." At the end of the third century B.C., a well known lord, Meng-Ch'ang,[12] who personally supported over three thousands house-guests, one day asked who would help him to collect some debts.

One guest named Feng Shuan[13] promptly responded, and the rich master ordered his servants to prepare a carriage. "Your Lordship," the guest politely asked before departing, "what should I buy after I collect all the money?"

"Buy anything you think I need," the lord responded casually.

Traveling for days, the guest reached the destined town and immediately assembled all the debtors. In a huge outdoor park, a few hundred shabbily-dressed and worry-stricken farmers, patiently waiting to present their reasons for delaying the payment. All of them were poor farmers and couldn't afford to repay the full amount.

Viewing this miserable spectacle Feng Shuan was speechless. Having accepted the duty to collect the debt, Yuan knew he could not return without the money. Yet these people obviously could not pay. Pondering his dilemma for awhile, Feng Shuan was struck with inspiration. After carefully checking and confirming each of the I.O.U.'s, he ordered his assistants to collect and burn all of the papers. He then turned to the crowd and proudly announced that due to the generosity of their master, this year's debts were totally exempted.

"Long life to the lord!" shouted Feng Shuan. With surprise and appreciation, farmers hurrahed in unison at the top of their coarse voices. This clever guest quickly returned to the lord's mansion. "You must be very capable," the master said, impressed by the swiftness of Shuan's return. "Did you buy anything special for me?"

"Yes, I did," the guest courteously answered. "Knowing Your Lordship has plenty of jewelry, well-bred horses, hounds, lands, houses, and other valuables far beyond an ordinary person's wildest dreams, I didn't think Your Lordship needed any material thing. Therefore, I decided to buy for you a 'gratitude.'"

"What is that?" questioned the lord. "I never heard of such item before."

"For many years," the guest continued "Your Lordship has focused on accumulating enormous wealth for your own enjoyment. On the other hand, even after a year's labor, those woeful farmers still couldn't pay their debts in full. The balance, compounded with high interest, would create even more debt, a vicious circle from which they could never be free. So on behalf of Your Lordship, I exempted their debts and canceled all of the I.O.U.'s."

The lord was shocked by this bold act, but remembered his own words, "Buy anything you think I need," and reluctantly accepted this vexatious fact.

One year later, in a severe political struggle, this lord fell out of favor. His servants fled, the "house-guests" disappeared, and his friends abandoned him. All of his properties were immediately confiscated and his life threatened.

Under a moonless night, with a chilly north wind gnashing at him, the lord, accompanied only by Feng Shuan and a few faithful servants, fled for his life from the capital city. They dared not to stop and traveled for days without rest. Running out of food, they soon found themselves on the edge of starvation.

While approaching a distant town at dawn one day, the lord observed with great amazement hundreds of people standing on the roadside, carrying meats, wine and other food and patiently waiting to welcome him. Soon his coach was surrounded. He stepped down and received the crowd, who submissively presented their provisions. Hurriedly consuming this welcome meal, the lord gratefully praised his house-guest. "Now, I understand the use of the 'gratitude,' which you bought for me last year."

Do small kindnesses on your hay days. You will have some faithful friends to help you out on your rainy days.

A Well-Known Thinker

Western Chou Dynasty
1100 B.C. to 770 B.C.

In traditional China the feudal system was rigorously enforced. People were constantly reminded to respect gods, nature, the emperor, their parents and teachers, in that order. In the eleventh century B.C., during the Western Chou dynasty, a nobleman named Tai-Gong Wan[14] received a lordship and was given a huge portion of land in eastern China. In his domain, there was a very famous philosopher, Hwa Shi,[15] who advocated absolute freedom and encouraged people neither to worship gods nor any authority. This philosopher had thousands of dedicated followers who treated him as a sacred prophet.

The newly-appointed lord, with sincerity, dispatched his ablest assistant to invite this philosopher to become an advisor, to help him in governing the people, or to accept some suitable academic position. In this way, the philosopher and his wild theory would be confined to the realm of the scholastic, and not infect the common people.

But Hwa Shi flatly and arrogantly declined. So the shrewd lord fabricated some serious crimes and promptly ordered his marshals to arrest this philosopher. After a brief show trial, he was condemned to death and executed shortly after. Citizens were shocked. This lord's high-handed behavior became a public embarrassment. He was immediately summoned back to the imperial palace and brought before the prime minister.

"How could you slaughter such a famous gentleman without proper justification?" shouted the prime minister. "His followers might cook up a riot."

After this reprimand, the lord responded "Your Highness, this person, who inspired people to be egotistic, is too well-known to be alive. With his fallacious and demagogic theories of self-indulgence, he neither wanted to be supervised by our laws nor be confined to any academic jurisdiction. His anarchical philosophy is counter-productive to our strict social system. Without proper supervision, he, with his charisma and a great ambition, could successfully spread those vicious germs of disobedience. First to be charmed would be a handful of unconventional intellects, who intend to have a voice in the world at all costs. Gradually, lower-level and undereducated clerks, grumbling about their meager salary, would follow suit. It would multiply with amazing speed. Then, illiterate farmers and labor hands might turn against us. In the long run, that man and his ideas would be extremely dangerous. If the number of followers grew big enough, they could threaten the tranquillity of our society, and our social system would collapse. Why wait till then and bet our necks on it? I had to snuff this potential crisis and terminate him for the sake of our dynasty."

Pondering for a while, the prime minister agreed with Wan and quietly sent him away.

CHAPTER 2

Avoid Future Problems

The Prophecy Becomes True

Tang Dynasty
618 A.D. to 907 A.D.

In a traditional society, people often used superstitions to rationalize the unexplained. An ordinary person's superstition would, at most, affect only a family. However, when an emperor was superstitious, the whole country might suffer dearly. This story took place at the end of the eighth century A.D.

One day, a man reported to Emperor Tang-Teh,[1] that a famous general, Bai Chi,[2] who had died over a thousand years ago, had appeared to him in a dream. The general informed this man that barbarians on the western border would soon invade their country.

The emperor was skeptical about this story, but as a precaution he reinforced that part of the frontier. In less than a month, barbarians actually attacked there, but were immediately repelled thanks to the army's increased readiness. Amazed, the emperor handsomely rewarded this person and intended to build a temple to commemorate this deceased general. With sincerity and enthusiasm, he discussed this matter with Prime Minister Lee Mee,[3] who was surprised by his master's lack of sophistication.

Acting seriously and holding back a smile with some difficulty, the prime minister pretended to ponder for a long while, and then spoke.

"Your Majesty, improving and revitalizing a country depends on the cooperation of people. The enemy was defeated by our competent generals and courageous soldiers. Their gallant behavior needs to be honored. If Your Majesty credits the victory to this legendary general, I'm afraid that the soldiers will feel indignant and ignored. Our servicemen's morale will be greatly dampened. Furthermore, to build a temple for him, Your Majesty is promoting superstition and ghost-worship. That will eventually destroy the self-confidence and self-reliance of our people, which is the most valuable resource that an emperor could possess. The consequences could be hazardous. By the way, I have heard there is a weather-beaten old shrine on the outskirts of the capital city which honors this general. To pay respects, Your Majesty could quietly send some servants to restore it, which won't cost much and will not raise people's suspicion." The emperor duly accepted this recommendation.

This prime minister was both farsighted and very sophisticated. Daring not to go directly against his master's naive idea, he objectively and diplomatically presented his opinions, step by step. He scrupulously upheld his own principles but shrewdly yielded on a few trivial points. For example, if the emperor didn't pay respects to this dead general at all and his army suffered a great loss in the next military encounter, this prime minister for sure would blamed and even lose his head because of poor advice. Therefore he cleverly advised his master to update a shrine, satisfying the emperor's simple-minded belief.

As an old saying goes; "When confronting a problem, it is much more reliable to seek help from one's self than from gods or ghosts."

Deal With The Wicked

Southern Sung Dynasty
1127 A.D. to 1279 A.D.

In the old days, eunuchs held a very unique position in Chinese society. They were typically undereducated or illiterate, and often came from extremely impoverished areas of the country. By castration, they could work in the political power center—the imperial palace—and had an opportunity to approach, win the trust of, and influence the emperor or his family.

Unlike the eunuchs, government officials were appointed by passing rigorous national examinations, which required tens of years of study and memorization of classical literature. They were always well-educated, and often looked down on the unlearned, upstart eunuchs. However, when an eunuch became influential enough to easily sway his master's opinion, which was not unusual in Chinese history, the officials had to flatter the eunuch to get their proposals reviewed by the emperor. It was a delicate and bitter relationship. This incident occurred in the middle of the twelfth century A.D.

Serving in the royal medical court, a notorious eunuch clandestinely sent many servants down to southern China to purchase well-trained carrier pigeons for his own personal purposes. Nobody knew the reason and all suspected Emperor Sung-Kao's[4] involvement. Rumors promptly spread.

Although this incident was swiftly reported to the palace, the emperor's reputation was at stake. Out of indignation, a hot-tempered, senior general immediately suggested that the eunuch's head be chopped off. A variety of other punishments were also proposed. However, a clever official, Chau Din,[5] advised otherwise.

"Your Majesty, this affair is not as simple as it seems on the surface. The real intention of this eunuch is less important than the effect of all this gossip and unrest. Our first objective must be to crush these rumors. If we don't discipline the accused eunuch, people will think, as gossip indicates, that Your Majesty dispatched him on a secret mission. Your Majesty's reputation will be greatly damaged. On the other hand, since we don't have any evidence of wrongdoing, we can't punish him. The best course, in my humble opinion, is to relocate the eunuch far from the capital city and start an investigation. After sifting through the whole situation, if he is innocent, we can receive him again. Otherwise, we can give him a fair punishment without being guided by gossip and innuendo." Pondering for a moment, the emperor accepted this recommendation and ordered the eunuch to resettle himself at once in a remote province.

In private, with great puzzlement and resentment, the general complained and questioned the official. "Why spare this rascal? He and his cronies are arrogant and unscrupulous. They deserve total extermination. If I could, I would torture and slaughter every one of those shameless swine."

"You don't understand eunuchs," the official calmly explained. "We know many of them are corrupt. However, if we behead this eunuch without a fair trail, we would alarm and alert the others. Thinking that we wish to destroy them all, they would unite against us. They might even influence the emperor and, for upholding their own interests, rescue their friend. But by removing him from the palace, the center of endless power struggles, we will please his peers and opponents who eagerly want to succeed him. If we wait, the absence of that eunuch will cause the others to brutally compete against one another. With the accused eunuch out of favor, he will be alienated by the others. None of them will re-admit him to their circles. We can sit back and enjoy watching these eunuchs weaken themselves as they jockey for position. After the whole investigation is over, even if it proves that the eunuch is innocent, on returning to the palace he will, to his distress, find out that his influence has been greatly reduced, if not totally destroyed by his rivals and peers." Laughing and applauding, the general shouted with joy and praised this official for his insight.

Divide and create contradictions among your opponents. You can sit back and watch as they compete with one another. Their internal dispute will eventually lead to their destruction.

Local Maps

Northern Sung Dynasty
960 A.D. to 1127 A.D.

We should encourage friendship and do our best to assist our friends. However, when too much cordiality might harm national security, we must draw a line. This episode happened in the middle of the eleventh century A.D. In that period, transportation was human legs or horseback. Printing was in its primitive stage. Maps were hand-drawn and primarily used for military purposes.

A team of Korean diplomats, on an annual visit, came to China's capital city to present gifts to the emperor. Passing through cities and towns, they courteously requested the local mayors or regional commanders to supply them with territorial maps. They claimed that they could study those maps for sightseeing along their route. As a gesture of good will, this solicitation, which had never been made before, was promptly granted.

Before approaching a mid-sized southern city, these diplomats sent the same request by messenger.

"I don't have one on hand. And, to tell you the truth, I don't even know how to prepare one," said Chern Shen-Jee,[6] a commander in the city. Feigning embarrassment, he suggested to the messenger "If you can let me see the other maps, I will be more than delighted to imitate them and draw one with similar details for you." The messenger returned and reported this to his masters. A few days later, the messenger came back with the maps that had been collected.

Accepting the maps, the commander immediately ordered his guards to burn them all, regardless of the astonished messenger's violent protest. The messenger was expelled from the city after a solid reprimand. This incident was abruptly reported to the central government. The commander was highly praised for his alertness and others, for their heedlessness, were punished according to the laws.

As an old Chinese expression says: If you hold your sword or spear at the wrong end, another person can easily grasp the handle and threaten your life with it. Giving maps to assist the foreigners on their trips, those local officials foolishly exposed the locations of mountains, rivers, harbors and other strategically important facts, which would have given potential invaders a military advantage.

With a Sense of Discreteness

*Northern Sung Dynasty
960 A.D. to 1127 A.D.*

Most people dream of a tranquil and wealthy life. However, a far-sighted man will feel uneasy about that tranquillity and wealth. Why? Allow me to present this case. In the eleventh century A.D. China was frequently disturbed by neighboring barbarians. One night while working late, the vice prime minister Wong Dan,[7] who didn't even have time to eat his dinner, sighed and murmured "Alas! The heavy load of work is killing me. Sooner or later I will die of exhaustion. When will our country enjoy peace again?"

"Oh, you are not joking, are you?" interrupted the prime minister Lee Hang[8] with a profound smile. "You should consider yourself lucky. Constant but manageable trouble is actually a good thing for a person as well as a country. With a few problems on our shoulders, we keep alert all the time. If the country eventually becomes peaceful, it will only develop hidden crises, which will be much more difficult to deal with in the future. After I retire, you probably will assume my position. At that time, our current skirmishes will most likely be over. Our country will be strong and prosperous. Our young Majesty will be spoiled by absolute power and carefree prosperity. Please, be aware of that."

Though disagreeing with his superior, the fatigued vice prime minister dared not to argue, and merely responded with a courteous nod. The far-sighted prime minister often deliberately presented all the current disasters, such as floods, fire, drought, or mutiny, to the emperor, who was frightened and dumbfounded.

"Your Highness," the vice prime minister privately asked, "Why should we present those misfortunes to annoy Our Majesty? In my humble opinion, it is not decent...."

"You are much in mistake," the prime minister immediately cut him short. "Our emperor is in his early teens, an age of innocent optimism. Without those calamities to constantly remind him that governing the dynasty is a demanding and strenuous job, I am afraid that Our Majesty will gradually become lax, and even neglectful of his duty. I will be retired very soon. It will become your responsibility. Be careful."

A few months later, the prime minister retired and the vice prime minister was promoted. Northern barbarians made peace treaties with China. Without war or other natural disasters, the national economy grew rapidly. The country enjoyed prosperity. With few matters of state to worry him, the young emperor began to visit famous mountains and rivers. Cunning eunuchs and crafty officials, who knew how to flatter their master, clandestinely approached the unsophisticated emperor and quickly won his trust. Favoritism developed. Regardless of their ability, unscrupulous power mongers employed their compatriots in government positions. Gradually, they occupied most of the influential positions. They encouraged the young emperor to build another grand-scale imperial palace and many extravagant mansions. The new prime minister was powerless to control this rapidly deteriorating situation. He wanted to resign but couldn't bear to watch the dynasty collapse. He then understood that his predecessor's farsighted concern had been most warranted.

A similar case happened in the chaotic Spring and Autumn period, 770 B.C. to 476 B.C. A strong country, after years of struggle and numerous bloody battles, finally conquered one of its equal-sized neighbors. The triumphant lord Gin-Li[9] intended to massacre every single one of the prisoners of war and enslave all of the citizens.

"Please, Your Lordship, for our own ultimate benefit, spare your enemy," a commissioner named Fan Shieh (Fan Win-Zye)[10] politely suggested. "Only an all-wise man could always keep a country free of troubles. For an ordinary statesman, there are always troubles either externally or internally. But by sparing our enemies, keeping them alive but weakened, we shrewdly create an opponent, which will constantly remind us of the importance of our self-existence and keep us alert. Otherwise, a carefree period will follow. We might become spoiled and even, if I may say, be destroyed by our own prosperity."

The lord sneered at this prediction and mercilessly ordered his soldiers to slaughter the conquered people and devastate the city. After this absolute victory, the country's reputation and prestige was at its peak. Ranking among a handful of the most powerful rulers, the lord became arrogant and wasteful. His people felt glamorized by their new status among the nations. They became egotistic and extravagant. Government became corruptive and citizens greedy. Lots of money was wasted in needless projects. As a result, heavy taxes were imposed on the laboring class, who had no political voice and suffered greatly.

During a period of natural disaster, many farmers, who couldn't pay their overdue taxes, rebelled against the government. Soldiers were called to handle them. Thousands of people died in the conflict. In another rebellion, the lord was murdered and his regime was overthrown.

An ambitious person must always possess a sense of discretion. He or she has to be fully prepared to confront any trouble, and to be aware of potential crises. Too much carefree living can gradually corrode discretion and eventually become a source of ruin.

We Manipulate It

Tang Dynasty
618 A.D. to 907 A.D.

In the late eighth century A.D., China was suffering through period of chaos and confusion. The emperor Tang-Teh[11] was a hostage to a handful of powerful and ruthless warlords. A well-known general, Lee Chan,[12] rapidly assembled tens of thousands of loyal infantrymen and indignant citizens and stationed this motley army on the outskirts of the capital city, which was under the rebel's control. This mixed army patiently waited for a proper time to start an assault to repossess this heavily-populated and well-constructed city.

In the old days, astrology was highly regarded and was very popular among educated gentlemen. The government had special posts for astrologists. Most educated people had some general knowledge of astrology. It became a custom before executing any important plan that the performer—from emperor, general, administer, civil servant, even ordinary people—would observe, study and interpret the specific movements of stars or hire an astrologer to do it. The astrologer would choose the best time to start the task, which people generally believed could bring good fortune and secure the success of this task.

Having waited for over a week, the army made no move. The soldiers were bored. The food supply was rapidly decreasing. Health conditions were deteriorating. There was rumor of a potential mutiny if this tedious and fruitless delay continued. All of the low-level officers were both depressed and distressed.

During this time, an astrologist approached the commanding general. "Congratulations, sir. Last night, I carefully studied the stars for hours and learned that you will win the coming battle in the next few days. Please, accept my premature but very sincere greeting...."

"Nonsense!" the general, obviously annoyed and disgusted, abruptly cut the astrologer short and scolded him. "How dare you, try to use superstition to butter me up? The existence of our dynasty is at stake. By all means, we must do our best to rescue Our Majesty. I don't give a damn about those twinkling stars."

Astonished, this aged astrologer, with embarrassment and uneasiness, grumbling for a moment, excused himself and left. A few days later, the general initiated a full-scaled attack. After winning several bloody military engagements, they finally recovered the capital city and saved the emperor. All of the commanders and assistants gathered to congratulate the general. One close associate, out of curiosity, asked him the reason behind his harsh reaction toward that astrologer's accurate prediction.

"Maybe you are too young to understand this. However, I can try to explain to you. There is something that we all know but couldn't comment on it," the general, with a profound smile, calmly explained. "I didn't rebuff him because of his forecast, but I am totally against him expressing it so publicly. As a common practice and a tradition, we indeed sometimes have our military plans correspond with the stars' movements. When it is favors us, we will boldly launch an assault. However, if I allowed our soldiers to comprehend this, I would totally forfeit the control of our army. If someday in the future an ill-fated sign was spotted in the sky, the soldiers would be scared, demoralized, and eventually lose their will to fight. Our army might collapse right in front of the enemy! How could we expect to win a war in a situation like that?"

"To keep that from happening, we must never place ourselves under the mercy of the heavens. We can use customs and superstitions for our own advantage but never allow it to upset our determination. To prevent my soldiers from relying on the stars, I had to openly deride the astrologer, although I privately agreed with him."

"Sir, you are really clever and farsighted," called his associate, and all his compatriots praised the general in unison.

A Voluntary Sucker

Ming Dynasty
1368 A.D. to 1644 A.D.

In this contemporary, material-oriented society, money is a symbol of success and prestige. However, it was not always so. In the old days, education was essential and money was regarded as an distasteful necessity. Chinese society was generally divided into four categories; intellectual, farmer, worker, and merchant. The goal of the educated class was to successfully pass three extremely competitive national examines and become government officials. Through step-by-step promotions, they might eventually high ranking positions, which carried both power and prestige, and could more efficiently serve the country.

On the other hand, for merchants, who were mostly meager peddlers, the expectation was totally different. Merchants were at the bottom of the social ladder, even those with lots of money. Laws prohibited them from wearing certain types of materials, hat colors, shoes, and jade. Even with wealth, they weren't truly respected by other levels of people. This small but interesting episode occurred in the late sixteenth century A.D.

In the capital city of Peking, an opulent merchant intended to move his family to a distinguished area of the city, where high-ranking officials had their homes. A real estate broker informed him that there was by chance a mansion available. The owner asked for 700 ounces of silver. After a brief inspection, the merchant, satisfied, promised to deliver the seller 1000 ounces of silver the next morning.

"Uncle, why be a sucker!" one of his nephews asked, hearing of the arrangement. "You could have had it for the original price. Why waste another 300 ounces of silver for nothing?"

The elder merchant laughed. "You don't understand how to do business at all, my nephew. In any business deal, you must be prescient, valiant and generous. The first rule of thumb is to get your objective accomplished at all costs. The price itself is merely secondary. My objective is to enter that neighborhood. The quality of the surroundings is much more important than the house. To be more precise, the neighbors' acceptance of us is critical for the family future. I am buying prestige and the recognition of our high-society neighbors. The owner, a retired high-ranking government official, could sell it to another gentleman of the same social status. Why favor me, a base-born and stinking-rich merchant? If I purchased it with 700 ounces of silver, I would invite endless problems. Other arrogant neighbors would be hostile to us. After we move in, they would complain, protest and isolate us. With the extra 300 ounces of silver, I more than satisfy the owner, who will speak well of us to our new neighbors. I will live there for generations to come. To secure a long-term tranquillity is much more important than the extra money, which will eventually be canceled out by coming inflation. Nephew, be farsighted and broad-minded. Never let money manipulate you. For a successful businessman, you must learn how to master your money. Spend it wisely and boldly for your ultimate long-term advantage."

Buy Your Own Fish

Spring and Autumn Period
770 B.C. to 476 B.C.

A competent prime minister, Gonsong Yee[13] very much enjoyed eating fish. Every morning, many people lined up at his front doors, eagerly presenting gifts of expensive and exotic fishes to him. Observing this, with great uneasiness, Yee calmly thanked them for their kindness but flatly refused to receive any one of those fish. This lack of social courtesy deeply surprised and annoyed his young brother, who lived with him. One night, after dinner, he curiously asked his elder brother for the reason.

"It's very simple," the prime minister revealed. "To avoid potential trouble, a wise man should never let his inclinations or hobbies be known by the public. I fail miserably on that point because my taste for fish is common knowledge. Knowing my likes, those gift-givers will try to satisfy them. If I accept their gifts, I owe them favors. When making a decision, I would inevitably or subconsciously have their concerns on my mind. I might bend a law to return a favor. If this continues, I risk getting caught and losing my position and reputation. Who then will bother to give gifts to a disgraced and powerless prisoner? Therefore, I must vigorously decline their generosity. Without owing them any gratuity, I am my own master. Making appropriate and unbiased decision, I can keep my post much longer and continue to buy my own fish." His brother promptly apologized for his shortsightedness.

Merit is earned, not given. So is success. There is no free meal in the world. One should always count on oneself, not anybody else, because others have their own interests in mind.

The Unfaithful Bodyguard

Yuan Dynasty
1206 A.D. to 1360 A.D.

When one's master betrays the country, what should one do? In the old days, the bond between servant and master was very close. This intimate relationship often lasted a lifetime, and even extended to their offspring. This episode happened in the middle of the fourteenth century A.D., near the end of Yuan dynasty.

In Canton, two ambitious men assembled tens of thousands of grumbling farmers and started to raid cities and towns. A local gentleman, Ho Zan,[14] rapidly reported this revolt to his governor and meanwhile collected a few thousand labor hands to cope with this chaotic situation. They had a few skirmishes with the rebels with indecisive result. The government duly dispatched several thousand well-trained soldiers, along with tens of thousands of local military forces. After many bloody battles, the imperial army repossessed territory after territory and eventually besieged the rebel's headquarters, a mid-sized city.

Killing one of the rebel leaders, the government soldiers encircled this city. However, the city was well-fortified, and the desperate rebels held off the army for months. To bring an end to this situation, Ho Zan publicly announced that he would provide a handsome bounty of eight thousand ounces of pure silver to whoever captured the other ringleader, a man named Wong Chen,[15] who was hiding in the besieged city with a few thousand diehard rebels.

A week after Ho Zan's announcement of a reward, the rebel ringleader was sent, heavily bound, to Ho Zan's camp by one of the rebel's own bodyguards.

"Look at yourself! How pathetic and helpless you are." the gentleman remarked in mockery. "Even your own servant betrayed you. How can you expect to accomplish anything at all when you can't even trust your own men?"

Shamefaced and sweating all over, Wong Chen dared not utter a word. After rewarding this bodyguard, Ho Zan ordered his assistants to prepare a caldron of boiling water and place it on a horse-drawn cart. Believing it to be prepared for himself, the ringleader shivered and trembled with terror. "Oh, by the way," called Ho Zan to the departing bodyguard, "you must stay here for a little longer." Several soldiers seized the man and brought him back to their master. Wrathfully staring at him, this gentleman, with obvious contempt, reprimanded him.

"You picked the wrong time to become so moral. Why didn't you turn yourself in and expose your master's conspiracy to the local authority while it was in the bud? You didn't do so because you wanted to enjoy the glory with your master. However, you didn't want to share the misery with him. What an unprincipled crook! By turning in your own master for a bounty when he was cornered, you instantly become a double-crosser, a heartless traitor who abuses your master's trust. Your disloyalty is the single most unforgivable crime any subordinate could possibly commit. I must punish you and teach other cunning servants a dear lesson. This spa is prepared for you, the betrayer."

With a gesture this gentleman ordered his servants to tie up this astonished bodyguard and throw him into the caldron, which would be drawn through some of the most crowded streets of the city. The unlucky bodyguard was slowly boiled alive while his crime was loudly and repeatedly declared on the road. From that day on, no servants dared to betray their masters.

Raise Pigs in the Palace

Northern Sung Dynasty
960 A.D. to 1127 A.D.

In the old days, the size of an imperial palace was so enormous that even an emperor might not visit every corner of it during his regime. This interesting story happened in the middle of the eleventh century A.D. The emperor Sung-Shen[16] was strolling around the royal garden and surprisingly discovered a pigsty. With astonishment and exasperation, he immediately directed one of his assistants to summon the responsible supervisor. Minutes later, the supervisor hurriedly arrived, and fell to his knees trembling with anxiety.

"What's wrong with you," the emperor sternly questioned "raising those filthy and stinking pigs in my royal garden, right besides these expensive and exotic flowers! Are you out of your mind? This is my imperial palace, not a shoddy farmer's vegetable garden. Why are these offensive animals here?"

"Your Majesty," the supervisor nervously explained, "it's not my idea at all. I didn't make this pigsty. It has been here for generations. They said that Your Majesty's ancestors built it and started this strange custom. I only faithfully follow it. We raise the pigs until they reach maturity. Then, we slaughter them and eat their meat. I really don't understand the reason behind maintaining this pigsty, but it is custom."

Shaking his head, the emperor allowed the supervisor to stand up and pardoned the man. The supervisor courteously bowed and backed away from his master. Still disgusted, the emperor directed his assistants to tear down that pigsty.

Several years later, one night in the palace, servants complained of a ghost appearing in a locked room. They testified that they saw some suspicious long shadows flying and floating there. An older servant said that fresh pig blood splashed all over the possessed room would effectively exorcise any evil spirit.

After an anxious search of the enormous imperial palace, all the servants and eunuchs reported that there were no pigs to be found. The incident was duly reported to the emperor, who suddenly recalled the sty he'd removed, and then understood the importance of having those pigs in the garden.

The emperor's ancestors were really farsighted. Although those pigs were never used, this measure of precaution was indispensable. The same mentality could also be applied to ordinary people. Without obvious and immediate troubles, you may ignore simple precautions that could have been of benefit in a future crisis.

An Uncommon Present

Northern Sung Dynasty
960 A.D. to 1127 A.D.

In the old days, to maintain a friendly relationship with its neighbors, China routinely exchanged presents with them. This amusing episode occurred in the early eleventh century A.D.

In a diplomatic communication, the country of Vietnam mentioned that they would like to deliver a live Kirin, a legendary animal of good luck, to the Chinese emperor next year. The Kirin, a symbol of fortune and prosperity, had never been seen before, and was known only through stories and in folklore.

If indeed the Kirin existed, it would be a magnificent gift and would bring great honor to the nation. But if this were a trick, China would be embarrassed in front of all her neighbors. Whether or not to receive this unusual present became a touchy issue. In a royal conference, the emperor asked his commissioners for suggestions. Most of the officials were silent. They truly didn't know how to handle this unique and delicate dilemma.

After a period of silence, Syma Guang,[17] the sophisticated prime minister spoke up. "Your Majesty, why should we be honored with such an unusual gift? According to mythology, a Kirin only appears in a country that is blessed. Since it appeared in Vietnam, it must be for them. We are not entitled to it. On the other hand, if this Kirin is fraudulent and we accept and worship it, we will make complete fools of ourselves. In either possibility, receiving it is not in our best interest."

"I understand what you are saying," spoke the emperor, "but what should I do?"

Syma Guang smiled. "We can use this incident to our advantage. Vietnam's real intention is no concern of ours. We must play along with them, treating this proposal as genuine and sincere. Your Majesty should publicly express your appreciation, but formally decline to receive this 'exceptional' present. Furthermore, Your Majesty should bestow on them a generous award for their thoughtfulness. As a result of this unselfish action, other neighboring countries will be deeply impressed and even surprised by Your Majesty's integrity and generosity. In the future, they will admire us for our selflessness and broad-mindedness, which is a gain for our dynasty's reputation. If this proposal is insincere or even mischievous, our southern neighbor will feel embarrassed upon receiving our lavish award."

After carefully listening to this perceptive suggestion, the emperor was delighted, and immediately instructed his diplomat to do all as the prime minister said.

CHAPTER THREE

Keep It Simple and Clear

You Can Have It

Tang Dynasty
618 A.D. to 907 A.D.

In the old days, the emperor was the single most powerful person in the entire realm. People treated him almost like a god. For example, when the royal coach passed through the streets there would be a brief curfew. Every resident had to stay at home with doors and windows tightly closed. Pedestrians hid themselves in alleys. Nobody was allowed to look at an emperor's face. An offender might lose his head. In some dynasties, harbingers were sent ahead to spread fresh yellow earth on the road, so that the emperor's coach would not touch the mundane and slovenly land.

In daily life, the emperor was surrounded by eunuchs and assistants. To gain the emperor's trust, which could be turned into influence, they sought ways to flatter him. The following two amusing episodes happened in the early ninth century A.D. A newly-enthroned young emperor named Tang-Wen[1] was on his way to a temple to one day honor his ancestors, which was a very important event for the new master. An officer came, knelt before him and reported that two wrestlers, waiting outside of his chamber, were ready to perform.

"What is this all about? Who hired them? I didn't order any wrestlers and I am in a hurry to attend the ceremony." the Emperor exclaimed.

"Your Majesty," answered a eunuch, "it is our tradition...."

"All right, all right, I know what they are getting at." the emperor impatiently interrupted, with obvious irritation. "Taking advantage of the situation, those two shameless swine expect to receive a handsome reward. Just let them wrestle in the front yard. After they finish, give them some money and let them go." He then departed without observing the game.

After this unpleasant experience, the 'tradition' was never again repeated. The smart emperor's disdain strongly conveyed a message, which was faithfully complied with by his shrew and observant eunuchs. Consequently, the master would never be accused of being radical.

Another day, while the emperor was watching a cockfight, a eunuch, who was well-known for getting attention and flattering his master, hooted and howled vigorously. Disgusted by this, his master coldly said to him "Well, it seems to me that you love those two cocks very much. I will give them to you if you can just keep your mouth shut." Profoundly embarrassed, the eunuch dared not to utter another word.

Although history generally labels this emperor as an average ruler, I think he duly demonstrated his sophistication and competence from those two interesting cases. Although the emperor was evidently against the practice of wrestling at that particular moment, he didn't publicly denounce it; thus evading a direct conflict with his eunuchs, a well-established and powerful special-interest group. Their potential threat must not be underestimated. Numerous historical tragedies show that notorious and power-hungry eunuchs ruthlessly murdered or dethroned emperors at their will.

But to respect his predecessors and avoid future complications, the emperor didn't openly condemn this faulty tradition, which was probably established in past ages by greedy eunuchs; rather, he cleverly chose to ignore it. Observing this, those wily eunuchs would clandestinely discontinue the practice.

In the second illustration, the emperor understood that the eunuch's behavior was definitely out of line. If he showed his anger and punished the eunuch, as any simple-minded and short-tempered emperor would do, he would, unnecessarily and erroneously, earn himself a notoriety for harsh treatment. On the other hand, if he ignored him, other eunuchs would consider him weak and feeble-minded and open to flattery. Contemptuously rewarding him with the cocks, the emperor cleverly revealed his disdain for sycophants while at the same appearing generous.

Absent-Minded or Forgiving

To snatch absolute power, an ambitious lord or a king would inflate a trivial quarrel with the imperial government as an excuse to go to war, and, after winning several battles, replace a weak emperor. To strengthen this attempt, the conniving lord would make friends with ambitious ministers working in the imperial palace, and acquire important inside information from them. To secure their own future positions, these ambitious ministers would collaborate with the power-hungry lord. But if the rebellion was unsuccessful, many high-ranking officials serving under the emperor would be arrested and beheaded due to their disloyalty. A similar episode occurred in the early first century A.D.

After many bloody battles, a rebellion was totally crushed. In the rebel leader's headquarters, imperial guards discovered several chests filled with thousands of letters revealing secret imperial information. Many well-known politicians' names appeared on those envelopes. If revealed to the public, their integrity and loyalty would be at stake. A bloodthirsty political purge was unavoidable. Glancing at them for a few seconds, those soldiers were shocked. Closing the chests and sealing them with official labels, they nervously reported what they had found and presented them to the Emperor Han-Kuan-Wu.[2]

Receiving those sealed chests, solid evidence of disloyalty, the emperor left them shut and urgently assembled all of his officials in the grand imperial hall. After brief but warm apologies for this unscheduled meeting, the ruler addressed the officials.

"Gentlemen, we all should take our ease and be delighted. We have completely destroyed the rebels. However, by chance, I notice that some of you are long-faced and suffering sleepless nights. At first, I was deeply puzzled and constantly asked myself. 'How come? What is bothering them? They should be more than happy to share the victory with me.' Now, I finally know the cause. Here is the cure."

He ordered his eunuchs to carry those chests out and lay them open in the front yard of the palace. Most of the officials were astonished, many on the edge of collapse, and nobody dared to utter a word. But to everyone's surprise the Emperor directed his guards to burn the letters. It was a generous and sweeping amnesty for those collaborators. All of the politicians, whether involved or not, felt greatly relieved. In their minds, they doubted no more; there would be no brutal and devastating political purge, which often affected innocents as well.

After that incident, those ministers deeply appreciated their master's benevolence. They respected him more than before. By his generosity, which spared many lives and prevented a costly and catastrophic political upheaval, the broad-minded and farsighted Emperor instantly won over numerous faithful subordinates, who had formerly been his secret foes.

Another similar case happened in the late fifth century, during the Southern Dynasties. After a brutal and critical battle between the imperial guards and rebels just outside of the capital city, an erroneous rumor spread that the rebel army had won the campaign and was marching towards the city. People were frightened. Many high-ranking officials and wealthy persons clandestinely snuck out of the city under a moonless night and visited the victorious advance detachments. To save their lives and secure their futures with the rebels, they brought money, foodstuffs, and cattle, and cordially presented them, along with their business cards, to those soldiers. The captains received those well-prepared gifts and business cards, as evidence of treason, and promptly delivered them to the headquarters. Hours later, several thousand fatigued soldiers entered the city and returned to their barracks.

In the morning, many worry-stricken people were assembled in the most popular marketplace. After climbing up one of the city's watchtowers, Hsiao Dau-Chen,[3] a senior general from the national guard, proudly announced their victory to the anxious residents, some of whom were more astonished than delighted.

"By the way," the general calmly added, "last night, my advance guards received a great many wrongfully-delivered donations and a few hundred business cards. They were for the enemy. Since the enemy was defeated and had fled, we kept and enjoyed those presents ourselves. Regarding those small pieces of paper, they are worthless to me. I will burn them up now."

Not even looking at those startled citizens, he ordered his aide-de-camp to build a small fire and throw the cards into it. The anxious audience deeply appreciated his broad-mindedness and shouted his name with admiration.

The main objectives of those two leaders were to uphold authority, and build a strong and tranquil empire for themselves and their offspring. This required all of their officials' undivided attention and absolute allegiance. A catastrophic political purge would be counter-productive towards a lasting victory. Perceiving this, each leader generously forgave their rivals, who in turn worked harder to scrupulously repay them.

Show Your Coolness

Northern Sung Dynasty
960 A.D. to 1127 A.D.

Traditionally, people believed that a muscular and well-built army commander was the best choice for the chief official of a border city. This might be correct when selecting a wrestler for a physical contest. However, to properly supervise an undereducated population and deal with unfriendly barbarians, a competent garrison leader needed intelligence and boldness, which are characteristics that can't be judged by physical appearance. Here is an interesting story which illustrates this point.

In the early eleventh century A.D., a government official named Lee Gi[4] was unexpectedly appointed to be a commander in a border city. This promotion surprised and worried all his friends and colleagues. Because he was slightly built and very reserved in his manners, they considered him to be too mild to deal with the hot-tempered generals who would be placed under his command. With indifference, this official quietly accepted this unusual assignment and started his tedious journey toward that remote city.

After weeks of travel he reached the border and was cordially welcomed by local businessmen and generals. Astonished by his insignificant appearance, they began to suspect his ability. After a few friendly encounters, his mild speech and quiet nature confirmed their suspicion. They firmly believed that their new commander was merely a political leftover, waiting for his retirement. Consequently, merchants rarely invited him to their social engagements. His generals and subordinates, who had earned their positions by winning many bloody and brutal battles, clandestinely looked down on him, ignored him, and treated him as a figurehead. Although they admired his education, they greatly doubted his ability to handle troops, and rarely discussed any military matters with him. But the Lee Gi was not offended at all. He would pass the hot and monotonous days by reading classical literature alone in his office.

One day in the city, a soldier robbed a woman in full daylight. He was promptly arrested and 'erroneously' sent to Lee Gi for a court-martial. As usual, Gi was casually reading a book. Putting the book aside, he asked the solider a few key questions, and the soldier blankly confessed.

Without hesitation, Lee Gi decreed that the solider should receive the death penalty. He wrote the order, passed it to his assistant and sternly ordered him to carry it out. Although surprised at his superior's swift conduct, the assistant directed three guards to drag the astonished offender out of the hall and behead him in the front yard. The whole trial and execution was over in less than an hour.

After writing the order, Lee Gi picked up the book and continued his study, as if nothing at all had happened. Observing this, his subordinates were struck with the realization that their commander was actually a top-notch and decisive leader, and they quickly spread this news around the city. The generals and local officials, after hearing this, were amazed by his swift and resolute action. From that day on, they started to pay respect to him.

Talk and speech are cheap and ineffective. Action counts. His behavior proved his ability and won the confidence of his compatriots.

Assign the Responsibilities   *Sung Dynasty*
                                            960 A.D. to 1279 A.D.

Everybody has a role to play. As long as you properly play your role, you shouldn't worry about the behavior of others. As an old saying goes; "Hold the tips of the collars. Then, shake for a moment. The shirt will naturally straighten." In other words, if everyone focuses on his or her own 'role,' the whole of society will operate smoothly. This amusing episode occurred in the Sung dynasty.

A government official named Fan Fon[5] was one day preparing a grandiose party in his mansion to entertain his colleagues. Since the guests would either be his superiors or his intimate friends, he was very nervous and frequently summoned his head cook, to quiz him about the progress in the kitchen. The host personally arranged the chopsticks and spoons many times. Standing behind him, one of his old servants showed a face of irritation, which was very unusual for him. Surprised by the frown, the anxious master asked about the cause.

"Sir, you are too fussy," the servant frankly remarked. "For a person to do big business, he must comprehend his limitations and assign appropriate responsibilities to others, then routinely inspect the results. If you become a prime minister someday, will you have time to single-handedly direct each of your tens of thousands of subordinates?"

"Of course not," said the master.

"Then please, if I may suggest, let your servants do their jobs — prepare the meal, set the table, make the house ready for your guests. You will then have more time to take care of your private affairs. It is a must."

With obvious embarrassment, the host thought for a moment, agreed with the servant, and sincerely thanked him for his valuable advice.

Replace the Lock

Northern Sung Dynasty
960 A.D. to 1127 A.D.

In the old days, China had an extensive boundary with less-cultivated northern barbarian tribes. Both sides had garrisons stationed at strategically important locations along their borders. The two countries' relationship was not always amicable, and military commanders often sought mischievous ways to humiliate their rivals without engaging in a battle. The following episode happened in the late eleventh century A.D.

There once was a city near the border, in a sensitive military zone. Due to a series of local disputes, the relationship between the two countries was sour. Vendors were prohibited from crossing the border to trade their merchandise. One evening, a night watchman discovered that the lock to the city gate was missing! He hurriedly reported this incident to the mayor, Liu Shun-Chin,[6] who seemed neither worried nor irritated. After a moment's thought, the mayor calmly instructed this night watchman to find an old, used lock to replace the missing one, and ordered the man not to begin any investigation.

The next morning, from the other side of the border, the barbarian chief sent a team of well-dressed representatives to visit the mayor. They were assigned to return the stolen lock, intending to mock the city's loose security and humiliate the mayor. Their visit was coldly received. After exchanging some dry words of greetings, they were escorted under heavy guard to city hall.

After a brief and wry speech, the chief barbarian representative, with diplomatic arrogance and derision, frankly expressed the purpose of their visit. But the quick-witted mayor pretended to be amazed. With contempt he retorted; "Poppycock! We didn't lose anything at all, not even a needle. What a dirty trick! Don't try to fool me. This piece of rust junk is definitely not ours. We didn't lose any lock at all. What a pathetic joke. Can you think of any other more creative ways to ridicule yourselves?"

The diplomatic delegation insisted on scrutinizing the city lock, and were allowed to do so. Examining the perfectly fitted and weather-beaten lock for a long while, they were finally convinced that the lock had never been removed. With great embarrassment they apologized, and were expelled out of the city.

Returning to their tribe, they indignantly described this humiliation to their chief, who was infuriated and severely punished the spy who had stolen the lock, believing him to be a liar.

Whatever is done can't be undone. However, quick thinking can change the odds to your favor. If you've suffered unexpected damage, your enemy would expect you to be anxious and frustrated. You must appear calm and relaxed, and pretend nothing at all has happened. This unperturbed behavior will baffle your enemy and create suspicion among them.

Cover Up the Damage

Northern Sung Dynasty
960 A.D. to 1127 A.D.

A case similar to "Replace the Lock" also happened during the Northern Sung dynasty. A vendor who lived near the frontier was walking alone one early morning on his way to the market. It was almost daybreak but the visibility was poor, and chilly night winds still hollered through the soulless street.

A suspicious shadow approached the vendor from behind.

Suddenly, he was attacked and knocked to the ground by an unknown hoodlum. The vendor looked up and saw the attacker's unusually muscular form and overheard his accented speech. Moaning and groaning, the man suspected that he was attacked by a barbarian.

After the attack, the offender swiftly snuck through the heavily patrolled border and returned to his tribe. The victim quickly reported this incident to a military commander named Lee Yun-Jer,[7] who gave the man some money for medical expenses and asked him not to reveal this misfortune to another living soul. The vendor agreed and was escorted home.

A few days later, a group of barbarian delegates came to this city for a good-will tour. One of them casually mentioned hearing about the attack. The commander vigorously denied its existence. Not having heard anything about it at all, the other officials indignantly and zealously joined with their superior's denunciation. The delegate demanded to review the military police's daily ledger, but no such incident was recorded there. With obvious astonishment, the delegate was embarrassed and hesitantly apologized for his misinformation. Returning to his tribe, he reported this 'misunderstanding' to his master.

At this time, the chieftain was cautiously weighing the credibility of some confidential military information newly acquired by one of his most competent spies. The spy proudly declared that he had successfully penetrated the heavily-guarded border and had hidden himself in the city for several days. During this time, he had some breath-taking adventures and eventually stole those valuable documents from the enemy's headquarters. On his return trip, he deliberately attacked an innocent passerby, assuming this offense would be reported and written down. This record would be proof of his bold statement and outstanding performance. The delegate's sole mission was to investigate and confirm the spy's declaration.

Receiving this undesirable report, the chieftain pondered for a long moment and concluded that he was defrauded by this spy. With frustration and resentment, he promptly discredited all the documents and clandestinely ordered the execution of that luckless spy, who never knew the cause of his extermination.

Unconventional Firewood

Northern Sung Dynasty
960 A.D. to 1127 A.D.

A high-ranking government official named Win Yan-Bo[8] was mayor of a populated south-western city. He enjoyed giving all-night parties. However, his servants, especially the body guards, hated these parties. The bodyguards were not allowed inside, and so had to suffer sleepless nights in the backyard garden. This was especially aggravating in winter, when the chilly night wind came screaming across the snow-covered land. Jamming themselves in a poorly-constructed shelter, the guards were not even allowed to build a fire. Despite heavy cotton uniforms, their bodies constantly trembled with cold.

On one occasion, the weather was intolerable. A bad snow storm was pounding the icy ground. Oblivious to the dreadful conditions outside, the mayor cordially entertained his guests in his warm and elegant mansion, while his bodyguards suffered through the storm. As the piercing winds howled around them, the bodyguards refused to bear such inhuman treatment anymore. Cursing and swearing, they angrily tore down a garden house and used the wood to build a huge campfire right in the middle of the mayor's backyard.

The light of this bonfire caught the guests' attention. Quickly discerning the possibility of an atrocious insurrection, they were frightened and dumbfounded. The party became deathly quiet. The stillness of the air tormented everyone's nerve. The guests felt like pigs and oxen in a slaughter house, waiting to be butchered at any moment.

Observing this, the host calmly remarked; "Never mind about that fire! It is really chilly outside. They deserve it. What an inventive idea! That garden house had deteriorated beyond repair. I was planning to hire some workers to take it down anyway." He then murmured a few words to his distressed housekeeper and sent him away.

"I have directed a servant to convey my gratitude." Everybody turned their heads toward him and carefully listened to his speech. "By the way," the host reminded his departing servant: "please instruct the chef to prepare some of his best dishes for those hard-working soldiers. And don't forget to bring wines, too."

The mayor then made a few humorous remarks and graciously encouraged his guests to renew their friendly conversations. In minutes, the party resumed its warm and playful atmosphere. It proceeded without any further disturbance. A conceivable revolt was cleverly avoided. After that party, the mayor never mentioned the incident again, though he carefully studied its causes and made the following changes; he shortened the duration and reduced the frequency of his parties and charitably improved the accommodations and utilities for the bodyguards. At first the guards feared a drastic reprisal, but after seeing the new arrangements, they truly appreciated their master's generosity and broad-mindedness.

Anger is like fire. If you inflame it with vexation, as firewood, the fire will grow wild and become an uncontrollable and devastating blaze. When confronted with insubordination, warm talk and sincere compliance could more efficiently win over one's subordinates than a high-handed and stern reaction. As an old saying goes "subdue your enemy with kindness." With tactfulness and self-control, the clever mayor deliberately laughed off the horrible menace and immediately met their reasonable requests. Focusing on the causes of the insubordination and then resolving them, he thoroughly extinguish the fire of exasperation and avoided a potential conflict.

An Unusual Punishment
                                                        Tang Dynasty
                                                     618 A.D. to 907 A.D.

In the powerful and prosperous Tang dynasty, China's economy was at an all-time peak. Merchants traveled thousands of miles and traded commodities with the Arabs and Romans. Due to peaceful politics, society rapidly progressed. This humorous story happened in a mid-sized city during those prosperous years.

In the old days, physical punishment was common for light offenses. But a newly-appointed mayor named Lee Fong[9] decided that caning, the most usual punishment, was cruel and unnecessary. So he exempted his civil clerks and replaced caning with a new method of discipline. From then on, if a civil employee was found guilty of a misdemeanor, they would no longer be caned on the back or buttocks. Instead, they had to wear a green turban.

A green turban had, and still has, a special meaning in Chinese society. The phrase "wearing a green turban" indicated that one's wife was committing adultery, which was extremely humiliating for the husband. The number of days the offender had to wear this embarrassing headdress depended on the seriousness of violation. The green turban was so noticeable that the offender could be easily detected, recognized, and sneered at. He would immediately become a laughingstock, and that stigma might accompany him forever. It was worse than a severe beating in the court.

The mayor's assistants urged one another not to mess around with the law. Most of them dared not risk their reputations on that physically harmless but publicly embarrassing punishment. During Lee Fong's mayoralty, the rate of lawsuits involving his subordinates was greatly reduced.

Confront with the Mutineers
Sung Dynasty
960 A.D. to 1279 A.D.

Picture this. You are a commander supervising several thousand soldiers. One day, you suddenly find yourself in the middle of a mutiny. Besides a few loyal bodyguards, you can command no one else. What will you do? There have been many insurrections throughout China's history, and most of the commanders fled for their lives. Their names became synonyms of cowardice and ignominy. But some generals reacted shrewdly and gallantly. They successfully appeased the rebels and won admiration for generations. The following example is one of the later.

Due to an unknown cause, the town garrison of a southern city suddenly had a mutiny. Rebellious soldiers marched out of their barracks, closed all the gates and started to loot the city. They burned public buildings and sacked rich residents' mansions. Hearing this atrocity, the mayor and the army commander swiftly deserted their posts and hid themselves in their well-secured residences.

The city was in chaos. Streets were littered with expensive clothes and jewelry. Fires were burning. With weapons in hand, unruly soldiers strode through the devastated streets, looking for trouble. Law-abiding citizens cowered in their houses, praying to be spared.

Nobody dared to interfere with the rebels except for one person. With some devoted marshals acting as bodyguards, a regional treasurer named

Shiue Charng-Ru[10] bravely approached the headquarters of the insurrection. In front of hundreds of ferocious soldiers who were waving their swords in the air, he dauntlessly began his speech.

"Gentlemen, you all have parents and wives, or children. And I am sure that you cherish them and their future as all ordinary people do." Pausing for a moment, the speaker waited for all of his audience to quiet down. With charisma, he sincerely continued; "Can anyone of you frankly tell me why you did this? This ignoble behavior will for sure disgrace your families. You will make them weep forever."

No one said a word. The military camp was as quiet as a graveyard. Shiue Charng-Ru knew that a fear of punishment might make the soldiers desperate. Observing this, the treasurer proceeded. "I fully understand that most of you are innocent followers taking advantage of the turbulent situation, or simply joining the herd out of curiosity and excitement. Turn yourself in now and save your own lives and your families' reputations. I will give you amnesty. Please, listen carefully. At this very moment, whoever drops his weapon, surrenders himself, and stands facing the wall, I will pardon him."

Impressed by his reasoning and grateful for his mercy, almost all of the soldiers threw away their swords at the same time and quietly followed the instructions. Only a handful of diehard ringleaders, nervously brandishing their weapons, defied the order. They dashed to a stable and galloped away on horseback. It was obvious that they caused this turmoil. A company of elite soldiers were selected, assembled, and fully armed. They were ordered to chase after and arrest the ringleaders. Hours later, on the outskirts of the city, in a small village, those traitors were encircled and, after a fierce skirmish, captured. The mutiny was pacified and the peace of the city was restored.

Open for Inspection

Tang Dynasty
618 A.D. to 907 A.D.

If someone asked you your life's goal, would you answer fame and wealth? If you achieve fame and wealth, what would you do then? The following story is about a well-known general who saved the Tang dynasty from total oblivion. For this distinguished achievement he became the second most powerful person in the whole empire. According to several similar cases in Chinese history, the few others who achieved such exalted status were not happy. At the pinnacle of fame and wealth, they became forlorn and power-less, easily falling prey to the jealous assaults of others. Furthermore, an emperor who was outshone by his 'mundane' subordinate would begin to worry that this subordinate might try to take the throne. Those 'living legends' found themselves caught between their subordinates' jealousy and their supe-rior's doubt. As a result, they and their families often suffered a premature death. So how could this general eliminate his master's suspicion? Here was his method.

In the late ninth century A.D., General Guo Tzy-Yi[11] had won countless battles over rebel armies and rescued the Tang dynasty from total collapse. Due to his outstanding performance, he was famous and greatly admired by the public. Naturally, this general became a living legend. Besides the emper-or, he was the single most powerful person in the whole country.

Like other high-ranking officials, Guo lived in a huge and well-adorned mansion with his family members and many servants. His residence occupied several city blocks and was more spacious than a public park. In traditional Chinese society, almost all of the mansions of the rich and powerful were built with high, thick walls and were heavily guarded.

Yet while all of his colleagues preferred privacy, the general deliberately kept the security around his property at a minimum. His grandiose front gate was unguarded. As a matter of fact, he didn't even hire a doorman, as other officials did. Visitors needed not identify or register themselves. They could come and go freely. Knowing his reputation, curious people often visited his residence, strolled in the beautiful gardens, and snooped around the bed-rooms. They treated his home as a public park.

One day, one of the general's junior associates was assigned to another location. The associate courteously came to say goodbye. With great aston-ishment, he discovered that his respectable superior was dressed in simple clothes, laboriously carrying a basket of water like a servant, and assisting his wife in putting on her make-up. Similar incidents had happened many times, and this bizarre behavior was immediately told all over the capital. Soon peo-ple were making jokes about this admirable general.

One day, the general's son bitterly complained to him; "Besides the emperor, Your Highness is the single most influential person in the dynasty. Could Your Highness act according to that status? Everybody laughs at us behind our backs. At least set up a checkpoint, as others do, at the front doors to regulate the rushing flow of human traffic. Our house is like a public zoo with noisy and curious strangers constantly coming and going as they please. Save us a shred of dignity, please. I beg Your Highness...."

"Don't be silly," said Guo. Beaming a mysterious smile, his father explained his behavior in a solemn tone. "You are still too young to comprehend that possessing enormous power can make you vulnerable, and that outshining the emperor is not a blessing at all. I am more popular than Our Majesty, which is very hazardous for our family. How many heroes in my awkward position have had a happy ending? Most of them and their family members were slaughtered because of their emperors' suspicion. The number of my foes equals the number of my friends. The later are silent and reserved associates, but the former are active and shrewd opponents. Because of jealousy, my political opponents will always secretly observe and meticulously investigate each detail of my life. They would love to see someone as eminent as myself forfeit everything, become penniless and even be beheaded.

"Any of minor error I might make could be blown out of proportion and become a great opportunity for a vicious attack on me. Taking me down, they for sure will be rapidly promoted and instantly earn Our Majesty's confidence. I have to be extremely careful about my behavior. In this mansion, there are over one thousand persons and five hundred horses. It is equal to a small-sized barracks. With Our Majesty's trust, I could fully enjoy my accomplishment and prosperity now. But who can predict the next emperor's attitude? Many officials and eunuchs have worked hard to dig up my blunders. If I built tall walls and monitored the visitors, as others do, my political opponents would certainly fabricate some far-fetched rumors to sabotage my reputation. After I lose my master's trust, my whole family's fate will be sealed.

"That is the main reason why I intentionally open the doors and encourage everyone to visit my residence. All my activities are clearly exposed to the public. That way, less vicious gossip develops. I do it for the long-term tranquillity of my whole family."

Deeply impressed, the general's son sincerely apologized for his own naive protest. A few months later, the reigning emperor died. As a custom to honor the emperor, all the people were forbidden to eat meat for several months. But the general's cook clandestinely slaughtered a pig. It was detected and reported. The general was immediately seized, detained and, after proper legal procedures, put into jail.

Peir Shiuh,[12] who conducted this arrest, was coincidentally, the general's former aide-de-camp, a loyal and trusted assistant. One of their mutual friends, during a social engagement, criticized him, in a tone of sarcasm.

"Didn't you remember our general's kindness? I am not sure whether you are absent-minded or heartless. How could you repay him this way?"

"Don't be ridiculous," the chief inspector retorted. "I will never mix my personal feelings with justice, as our general taught me when I was a young military officer. That is why I always respect him, a fine and polished gentleman. If I, with good intentions, foolishly covered up this petty violation for him, I would be doing him a greater harm. Other officials who envy his fame and position, will reveal this with exaggeration to the new emperor. The consequence will be undesirable or even devastating to our honorable general. And I firmly believe that he will agree with my conduct." Pondering for a moment, the friend, with obvious embarrassment, apologized for his thoughtlessness.

Living under a master of absolute authority, a man with enormous power and fame, besides being humble and polite, has to be prepared for all sorts of inspection and criticism. Sometimes it is not a blessing to outshine your superior.

CHAPTER 4

Wedge Your Way In

According to Similar Cases

*Southern Sung Dynasty
1127 A.D. to 1279 A.D.*

Have you ever been faced with such an unpleasant experience? Under intimidation, you are forced to say something totally against your will. Could you express some words that are so vague that it could be interpreted both ways? I believe most people couldn't do that. However, with diplomatic shrewdness, a prime minister from the Southern Sung dynasty did it and saved both his neck and integrity.

After a successful palace coup d'etat, a band of rebels controlled the capital city and held the emperor hostage. However, their conspiracy was not completely achieved. Stationed nearby, commanders and generals were busy mustering soldiers and preparing a full-scale counterattack to recover the city and rescue their master. Realizing that their motley forces were far inferior to the well-equipped national army, rebel leaders were scared and anxiously negotiated terms with the detained Prime Minister Ju Shen-Fay,[1] who was clever and sophisticated.

After hours of dialogue, they finally reached an agreement. First, reinstate Emperor Sung-Kao[2] at once. Second, pardon all the dissenters. Third, appoint the 'radical' leaders to be governors. Fourth, immediately disband all the newly-assembled rescuing troops. All of those conditions were properly executed. With delight and satisfaction, the rebel leaders promptly released the emperor, who reluctantly commissioned them as governors in outlying province.

All the residents and government officials urged the insurgents to leave the war-torn city as soon as possible. A wily rebel assistant suggested to his masters that they should also demand gold plates of amnesty to further secure their safety.

"What a brilliant idea!" the leaders agreed. Gathering their troops before departure, they visited the imperial palace, confronted the emperor and demanded a carved proclamation granting them amnesty, without which they refused to leave. The emperor was furious and didn't utter a word, only stared at them with abhorrence.

"Of course we will," the shrewd prime minister promptly cut in, saving his master from suffering a total humiliation. With the emperor's acquiescence, he rapidly wrote; "According to similar cases, an appeal of clemency is duly granted." The rebel leaders were more than satisfied and happily marched all of their insurgents toward the assigned province, leaving behind a few companies, as rear guards, to patrol the city.

The next day, an official came to see the prime minister. "Your Highness, I don't understand this order," he said, presenting the paper.

"Did you check the files?" the prime minister mildly asked.

"Yes, Your Highness," he answered, "but I couldn't find any similar case at all...."

"Then," the prime minister grinned and remarked "You should know how to handle this situation." Laughing, they concluded this dialogue.

The gold plates were not issued. The emperor never pardoned the rebels. Their forces were annihilated by government troops in less than six months.

If the prime minister had unwisely quarreled with the rebels, either his head would have been chopped off or he would have eventually acceded to their demands. But as a master of the art of language, he was sophisticated enough not to directly irritate the rebels. He neither broke his promise, because he didn't make one at all, nor damaged the country's reputation. Under force of intimidation, he couldn't ignore the rebel leaders' requests. However, by seemingly accepting, but actually rejecting, their demands, he gave an answer which appeased them and satisfied the emperor.

Divide Among Sons

Western Han Dynasty
206 B.C. to 25 A.D.

In the old days, beneath an emperor, was a handful of kings and lords. Their domains were huge and prosperous. Sometimes an ambitious prince, on becoming king, would secretly accumulate weapons and arms to rebel against and replace a weak emperor. Confined in his well-decorated imperial palace, how could an emperor know what other kings contemplated? Were they growing in power? Might they threaten the tranquillity of the empire? These thoughts would constantly haunt and irritate a mediocre ruler, causing him to suffer many sleepless nights. The following conversation took place in the Western Han dynasty.

In the first century B.C., young Emperor Han-Wu[3] was alarmed about the expanding powers of his kings and lords. Tormented by this anxiety, he asked an assistant Zufu Yan[4] what could be done about this.

His assistant said "It is very simple. Without spending a penny and wasting a human being, Your Majesty can weaken their authority. Each lord has many sons and daughters. Your Majesty could ask that the lords divide their realms equally among all their children, rather than bequeath their entire domain to the oldest son, as is traditionally done. Your Majesty could then award princely titles to those children, which they will appreciate.

"Gradually, the lords' territories will diminish and their authority will dwindle. Your Majesty will be respected by the newly-created princes and won't need to worry about the lords' increasing powers anymore."

Hearing this advice, the emperor praised his assistant for this innovative idea.

Accompanied by Opponents

Tang Dynasty
618 A.D. to 907 A.D.

In the old days, people thought some mountains and rivers were blessed. To uphold the prosperity and tranquillity of the empire, rulers were required, as a sacred duty, to personally visit Mountain Tai, located in what is now Shantung province, a few thousand miles away from the capital city. This royal voyage was very costly. Tens of thousands of servants and imperial guards would accompany their master. The cost of this journey, ironically, would burden the national treasury for years to come. Furthermore, when an emperor was away from the imperial palace, how could he be sure that the unfriendly and cunning northern barbarian tribes wouldn't take advantage of the situation and invade? A dilemma such as this occurred in the Tang dynasty.

In the early eighth century A.D., Emperor Tang-Hsuan[5] was going to visit Mountain Tai. A journey of several months was expected. He worried about the security of the northern border, fearing that barbarians might invade while he was absent. He requested the Defense Minister Peir Gwn-Tin[6] to strengthen the extensive border.

"Your Majesty," the minister responded, "visiting Mountain Tai is a glorious event. This trip will show that our country is both wealthy and strong. But if we increase the numbers of soldiers on the northern border, the barbarians there will interpret this as a sign of fear and sneer at us. Besides, it is very expensive to do that. This added expense, combined with the cost of your journey, might overburden our national treasury,"

"What should I do?" the emperor moaned. "I can't risk our national security for this expedition."

"Your Majesty," the minister continued, beaming a profound smile, "there are several barbarian tribes. The mightiest of those tribes is seeking to improve relations with us by marrying one of our princesses to their ruler's son. Though we haven't agreed to it yet, as a gesture of good will, Your Majesty could send a delegate to invite their chieftain to accompany you on this respectable journey. Other less powerful tribes also want to be included. Then we will become friends and there will be no possibility of military friction. By doing this, we don't need to reinforce our border, which will save us money. Also, we can duly demonstrate our wealth and prosperity to the barbarian rulers, which will greatly dishearten their invasion intentions. Finally, by having those "guests" at hand, we are certain there won't be any border conflict. Consequently, our national security is ensured. Without extra cost, Your Majesty's worry is resolved."

The emperor was well pleased and did all his minister advised. The barbarian king and other rulers delightfully accepted this honorable invitation. Their participation insured the tranquillity of the border. By not dispatching extra troops to the boundary, the emperor saved a great deal of money and maintained the country's dignity as well.

With a little creative thought, one can cleverly turn a dilemma into an opportunity.

Receive the Contribution
Tang Dynasty
618 A.D. to 907 A.D.

Picture this. Someone very well-known for mischievousness promises to give you an expensive gift. Would you be puzzled or pleased? If you agreed to accept the gift, you might be teased or even humiliated by its falsehood. On the other hand, if you declined this hospitality, you would for sure irritate the donator and jeopardize the poorly-maintained relationship. How would you react? There was a similar episode, on a much larger scale, during the Tang dynasty.

In the late eighth century A.D., the Tang dynasty was in decline. Powerful warlords dominated politics by holding up local taxes and raising their own armies. Acting as rulers in various independent states, these warlords rarely paid any respect to the central government and personally transferred their authority to their oldest sons.

The emperor, Tang-Teh,[7] one day, surprisingly received a cunning warlord's report indicating that he would like to contribute three million dollars to the imperial palace. During peace time, this behavior would be interpreted as a deed of allegiance towards the dynasty. However, this warlord was notorious for his arrogance and dishonesty. The emperor was deeply distressed. If he agreed to receive the money and it turned out to be mere a false promise, the emperor would be humiliated. Furthermore, he might have to visit there to get the money and be held hostage by this power-hungry and ruthless warlord. He would lose both his head and the dynasty.

On the other hand, if he courteously rejected this contribution, he certainly would aggravate this short-tempered donator, who might use this rejection as an excuse to agitate his people to overthrow this 'egotistical' monarch. A rebellion was possible.

Worriedly strolling in the imperial palace, the emperor knew he didn't know how to deal with this dilemma and abruptly summoned his prime minister, Tsuei Yo-Fu[8], to discuss this delicate matter. After a long exchange of opinions, they finally concocted a plan: to boldly accept the warlord's 'donation' at face value, and then endow it to the warlord's soldiers, under the emperor's name. The emperor dispatched a trusted censor to faithfully execute this order, which was speedily carried out.

This dilemma was cleverly resolved in favor of the emperor. First, he out-maneuvered his foe and rightfully earned a name for shrewdness. Second, the dynasty's reputation was maintained. Finally, the warlord must pay the full amount, otherwise he would foolishly defraud his own soldiers, who by all means would appreciate the emperor for his generosity.

Receive the Foe's Gift

Later Chou Dynasty
951 A.D. to 960 A.D.

This incident happened in the middle of the tenth century A.D. China was unfortunately divided into several countries. Unification attempts often resulted in wars between these countries. Some rulers attempted to use money to corrupt the relationship between an opponent's leader and his generals.

Once, the most powerful northern dynasty sent one of its generals on a diplomatic mission to an opulent southern country. After accomplishing his assignment, this general, Tsaur Bin,[9] prepared to leave. The host king unconventionally invited him to his palace, cordially chatted with him for hours, and granted him some very expensive presents. The general flatly declined to accept them. Leaving the country in a boat, the general was chased and stopped by a southern diplomat, who brought those presents and insisted on giving them to him. Shaking his head, the general smiled bitterly and remarked "I would be damned if I refused it this time."

Arriving in the capital city, he immediately turned in the presents and meticulously reported this incident to the Emperor L. Chou-Shih,[10] who was very pleased and permitted the general to keep them. To avoid any future suspicion, the general then deliberately handed out these gifts to his relatives and subordinates, and didn't keep a penny for himself. Overhearing this, the emperor was deeply impressed, and trusted the general even more than before.

Those treasures didn't achieve their original purpose—creating suspicion between the general and his master. On the contrary, it helped the general, due to his own openness and generosity, to fortify his relationship with the emperor. Ironically, a few years later, the same general led troops to invade, battle and eventually conquer this wealthy but weak southern kingdom.

Honesty earns trust. And the prelude of honesty is openness, which is the only way to eliminate doubt.

Turn Themselves In

In 1457 A.D., after a successful coup, the emperor was restored. A few months later, according to recently discovered evidence, there were several thousand persons who had taken advantage of the chaotic situation and been either wrongfully promoted or rewarded. Informed, the emperor was very displeased and summoned his prime minister Lee Shan[11] to discuss this matter. Upon arriving, the visitor was instantly briefed.

After a moment of consideration, the minister sincerely suggested, in a solemn tone "Be extremely cautious, Your Majesty. Our country just suffered a catastrophe and couldn't bear another one. If we start to arrest all these speculators now, other innocent persons will be needlessly frightened. Out of nervousness, they might misinterpret it as a brutal political purge. On the basis of an unfortunate misunderstanding, they may revolt against us. In seeking justice, we foolishly trigger another commotion. Furthermore, those real lawbreakers will certainly defy and resist our arrest, initiating a rebellion against the country. The consequence will be devastating. However, if we allowed this affair to quietly blow away, those offenders would certainly look down on us. Either procedure is not for our best advantage."

"What a pain in the neck!" the emperor hopelessly shouted. "I can neither overlook nor punish them. What a dilemma! How should I handle those spineless crooks?"

"Don't worry, Your Majesty." Beaming a profound smile, the prime minister confidently continued. "They didn't commit any atrocious or unforgivable crimes. They are merely greedy. Your Majesty could give them an opportunity to turn themselves in and repay all the rewards. In doing so, Your Majesty would cleverly demonstrate your sophistication and broad-mindedness. Under such an unfavorable and embarrassing situation, I believe that they, at least most of them, dare not to defraud Your Majesty again. The few exceptions will be easy to deal with later, and potential turmoil can be avoided."

Pondering for awhile, the emperor agreed and announced the decree the next day. Knowing that their falsification was unveiled, the swindlers realized that if they didn't surrender themselves now they would face serious punishment. Over four thousand people confessed and returned their rewards. After signing some legal papers, they were immediately pardoned. Without losing single human being, the government resolved this problem and upheld its reputation.

As a famous military strategist once remarked, "Never charge a cornered enemy at once. To save their necks, they become brutal and dauntless. If you do, your casualties will be high. You should let them know their hopelessness then patiently persuade them to give themselves up. If you succeed, your losses will be at a minimum, if any." Although that is good military strategy, it can also be applied to interpersonal relationships. Before reaching any judgment, you must always carefully weigh an offender's intention. A severe punishment is not necessarily the most efficient discipline, and its fiendishness may frighten others. To avoid similar castigation, they may commit even worse crimes.

Outwit the General

Ming Dynasty
1368 A.D. to 1644 A.D.

In the early sixteenth century A.D., Emperor Ming-Wu[12] was accompanied by a notorious general Jean Bin,[13] who was actually kidnapping his master, on a visit to southern China. On the return trip, fatigued and sick, the emperor fell into a coma. He could die at any moment. His faithful prime minister, Young Tin-Ho,[14] and other commissioners had clandestinely prepared to arrest this traitorous general.

But the general, a capable military strategist, was escorted and protected by more than one thousand diehard and muscular bodyguards, and the possibility of successfully overpowering them was slim. If the ministers allowed this opportunity to slip away, the general would soon go back to his domain, where he commanded several armies. He for sure would become a powerful overlord and threaten the dynasty.

"We must outsmart this malicious ass here and now." said the prime minister.

Pondering for a moment, a shrewd commissioner named Wong Choung[15] remarked, "Ushering Our Majesty to here, the outskirts of the capital city, those bodyguards of his accomplished their sacred mission. They deserve a handsome reward. However, the location where the reward will be distributed must be far away from their barracks. While the soldiers swarm to accept it, we can storm the headquarters and capture this general. With the element of surprise, we can minimize our casualties and maximize our chance of success."

The others agreed to the plan and announced the award the next morning. The bodyguards were delighted. They happily left the city and marched over fifty miles to collect their prize. In a few hours, most of them were gone. The prime minister personally conducted a few small groups of dedicated servants to attack. Without confronting any noticeable resistance, they overpowered a handful of guards and successfully arrested the general, who was completely surprised.

Mountains are the playground of tigers, and so are oceans to sharks. However, when out of their environment, they become defenseless. For a demagogue, people are his most valuable asset. Out of the crowd, he is nobody. A capable general needs to have well-trained soldiers to demonstrate his military genius. Without them, he will instantly become both powerless and vulnerable.

An Important Letter

Northern Sung Dynasty
960 A.D. to 1127 A.D.

In the old days, an emperor could have hundreds or even thousands of concubines. Their sons would receive titles as princes. One of them would eventually succeed his father and become the new ruler. However, he was often not the empress's real son. As a result, the relationship between prince and empress was frequently unemotional or even cold. This petty discrepancy might turn into an internal dissension. With agitation, the consequence could be devastating.

One such situation occurred in the middle of the eleventh century A.D., during the Northern Sung dynasty.

The newly-enthroned Emperor Sung-Ying[16] didn't pay much attention to the empress dowager, who was not his natural mother. She, a strong-willed woman, had enjoyed fame and popularity for over thirty years and couldn't tolerate this aloofness. One day, she clandestinely dispatched a letter to Prime Minister Han Chi,[17] who was the single most powerful man next to the emperor. In this letter, she fastidiously criticized the ruler's negligence and irresponsibility toward her. At the end, she boldly wrote. "Sir, consider my husband's kindness and the tranquillity of our empire. Please help and save me, a weak and miserable widow." In China, those words often implied initiating a coup.

Pretending nothing unusual, the prime minister quickly read through it, accepted the letter, and politely sent the courier away, who had been ordered to wait for an answer. Expecting to obtain a written response, the messenger, with obvious puzzlement, left empty-handed. The official immediately made an urgent appointment with the emperor, which was granted. In hours, they met alone in a chamber, without any servants or assistants.

After brief amenities, with a solemn expression the visitor said "Your Majesty, please, don't be astonished by what I have to tell and show you. I have a letter which concerns Your Majesty. Please, never reveal its content to another living soul."

After this precaution, he courteously approached and presented the letter to his master. The emperor carefully read the letter and was enraged.

"Allow me to proceed." The prime minister continued. "The empress dowager never gave birth to a son. She helped Your Majesty to win over the late-emperor's trust. Without her, Your Majesty would still be a prince. Please, never forget her kindness. As long as Your Majesty pays a little more attention to her, I believe it will contribute to our dynasty's peace and prosperity."

Pondering for a moment, the master remarked, with appreciation, "Thank you for teaching me this." He then handed this letter over to this official. "I dare not keep it."

With astonishment, the prime minister declined. "Its existence is greatly harmful to our country. If someone with political ambitions accidentally got hold of this, they could fabricate some excuse and agitate the people. A crisis with destructive consequences might be unavoidable. Please, Your Majesty should destroy it immediately. Then, this matter is closed forever." Agreeing with him, the emperor placed the letter over a candle and burned it.

From that day on, the emperor and his wife started to have more social contacts with this lonely, aged empress dowager, who was delighted. She was often invited to be an honorable guest at traditional celebrations. Their relationship rapidly improved. No one ever noticed that there had been any disagreement. A trivial family dispute, which could easily have become a destructive civil war, was quietly and cleverly eliminated.

PART TWO

Sagacious Wisdom

Since the beginning of the universe, the world has been divided into two parts—the vaporous air and solid earth. A day is divided into bright daylight and dark nightfall. Likewise, people can generally be classified as either smart or slow.

Place a lighted candle on a table and it lights only a room. The sun, hanging in the sky, casts its light over mountains and rivers. Therefore, knowing how to position oneself is very important. The success of a person with profound knowledge and far-sightedness is almost predictable. On the other hand, a sightless man riding a blind, crippled nag to the edge of an icy cliff is sure to meet his doom.

While a smart person foresees outcomes, a slow person doesn't even know what is happening. A fool daydreams of impossible success or worries about the unknown while an ambitious person, through repeated effort, achieves goals. One who possesses sagacious wisdom can glean an opportunity in a crisis, and earn a fortune amid total destruction. No matter how bad a situation becomes, the smart will always benefit. Here are some stories, in four categories, exemplifying this principle.

CHAPTER FIVE

Keen Perception

With Ivory Chopsticks

Shang Dynasty
1766 B.C. to 1122 B.C.

When observing something unusual, you must be alert. If, for example, you noticed one of your poor friends suddenly becoming an extravagant spender, you would be curious and try to discover the cause of that change. A cautious person could perceive and scrutinize any trivial difference then make a projection and react accordingly. This interesting episode occurred during the eleventh century B.C.

In ancient times, commerce and technology were at their primitive stages. People lived in an agrarian society. Tools and utensils were for practical use, and had no decoration. Emperor Shang-Jow[1] one day began using a pair of ivory chopsticks to eat his meals. Gee Tzy,[2] his brother, who was famous for his wisdom, saw this and sighed deeply.

"The dynasty is doomed." he whispered to himself. "Our Majesty won't match his ivory chopsticks with ordinary earthen dishes. A costly wine cup made of rhinoceros' horn will be considered merely proper. Nobody who dresses in simple clothes and lives in a shabby lodge uses ivory chopsticks to eat grains and cereals. Everything, from clothes to house, has to be excessively luxurious to match them. Unfortunately our country is built on agriculture, a less than wealthy society. We can't afford any luxury at all. If we waste too much money on personal enjoyment, our neighboring countries will grow envious, invade and conquer us. Oh miserable people! You will either be slaves of your own avaricious emperor or of an ambitious enemy. No matter who rules—war, poverty, and chaos are merely around the corner."

Less than a year later, the emperor ordered hundreds of thousands of farmers to build several grandiose palaces and well-furbished gardens for him.

For years the citizens suffered miserably while the emperor lived lavishly. Then an ambitious lord from the western region challenged the emperor and, after winning several important battles, overthrew the dynasty. The greedy ruler was forced to commit suicide by burning himself alive, accompanied by some of his most favorites concubines, on a high tower of his gilded mansion.

Mundane people love to entertain themselves with an extravagant lifestyle. As a person of responsibility, you must not live beyond your means. Then, you will never have any financial difficulty. Besides knowing and managing yourself, you must also be watchful of the outside world. As an old saying goes, "Always be aware of any sudden change." Besides detecting a change, you must analyze the origin of its causes, and estimate and theorize its consequences. Then you can act appropriately and not be surprised by a coming calamity.

The Real Reason

Western Chou Dynasty
1100 B.C. to 770 B.C.

Often you can learn much more from a person's actions than from his words. A king who established the Western Chou dynasty discovered this fact three thousand years ago.

After winning a few decisive battles, King Chou-Wu[3] overthrew the Shang dynasty, took power, and became the emperor. One day, overhearing that there was a wise man who dwelled in the capital, the new emperor decided to pay the man a visit, accompanied by his trusted assistants. After hours of searching, they finally located the man.

Gently knocking at the door, which was promptly answered, the emperor disclosed his identity. The wise man courteously conducted the ruler into his shabby lodge. Many curious bystanders swarmed around, keeping a distance, and watched with interest.

After brief amenities, the noble visitor politely asked the wise man about his opinion of the causes of the last dynasty's collapse. Pondering for a moment, the man said he could not answer that question right away, and suggested that the emperor come back tomorrow. The emperor agreed.

The next morning, the emperor arrived punctually. Knocking at the door, he received no answer. After patiently waiting for a few moments, the emperor began to be disturbed. Then some neighbors told him that this old man had fled the house last night in a hurry. The emperor felt cheated and betrayed.

"Your Majesty," his prime minister Chou-Gong[4] remarked, "I believe I know the reason. He is indeed a fine, old-fashioned gentleman, who didn't want to openly criticize the last emperor, who technically was his master. By intentionally breaking his promise with us, he cleverly conveys some of the most important causes of the previous dynasty's downfall. I think his deliberate absence indicates that trust and credibility are essential for the prosperity of an empire. Abusing both, the previous emperor lost his huge dynasty as well as his precious life. Your Majesty must always keep that in mind."

The emperor agreed with this perceptive analysis, and with satisfaction they left.

Nobody truly knew about the wise man's real intention. Debating whether the prime minister was either quick-witted or far-sighted is unimportant. His analysis was both logical and persuasive. The new emperor, a warm-hearted and energetic ruler, delightfully accepted and faithfully followed the prime minister's interpretation, which was very rewarding for him and his offspring. His dynasty lasted over two hundred years.

Accept the Award

Spring and Autumn Period
770 B.C to 476 B.C.

If you were entitled to an award but really didn't want it, should you courteously decline it? The all-wise philosopher Confucius's answer was "No." Why is that? This story, which happened in the sixth century B.C., tells why.

Due to the deterioration of the Eastern Chou dynasty, China was split into a handful of independent political regions. Seeking to expand their territories, these countries often battled one another. To pay off the huge costs of war, the winning country sold captured soldiers and citizens as slaves.

Suffering dearly on recent military engagements, a mid-sized country located on the Shantung peninsula had drained itself of both men and natural resources. National security was in jeopardy. To offset this problem the government made a decree: Whoever is free and brings back a prisoner from a neighboring country will be rewarded.

During a business trip to another country, a rich merchant named Tzy Gon⁵ discovered that one of his countrymen was working as a slave in a factory. Out of sympathy, he purchased the man and brought him back to their own country. The man was released and became a free citizen again. According to the law, the merchant should be rewarded. But when local officials presented the award, the merchant cordially declined to accept it.

"You are much in mistake," said Confucius, his teacher. "Your rejection will greatly discourage others from receiving the reward. From now on, nobody will actively help to save those prisoners from misery. Because you made an exception, other people, to uphold their reputation, will have to do the same. Without a reward as a stimulation, those rich merchants will be reluctant to do the kindness. I know you are wealthy and neither need this meager reward nor the glory. However, others are eager to have them. Accept the award and then donate it to the poor. Please, never bend a rule to fit your own personal inclination. Other people will have difficulty in following it." Considering this for a moment, the merchant sincerely apologized for his thoughtlessness and went back to receive the award. For fame and recognition, other merchants generously followed suit. Many prisoners regained their freedom this way.

Over-Patriotic Persons

Spring and Autumn Period
770 B.C. to 476 B.C.

If someone is so loyal to you that he would cook his own son and castrate himself for you, would you still doubt his allegiance? Unfortunately, the answer is yes. A sagacious master will be suspicious of the true intentions behind extreme shows of loyalty. A similar episode happened at 645 B.C.

The Eastern Chou dynasty was powerless. Its existence was in name only. China was actually split and unfortunately divided into several politically independent states. A handful of ambitious 'lords' dominated the whole empire. Regardless of title, they acted as monarchs in their own domains. And they were frequently at war with one another to expand their territories. A powerful lord Chi-Huan,[6] one day visited his prime minister Goan Jong,[7] who was on his deathbed.

The prime minister had helped his master to build their state from scratch. Being one of the most influential rulers, the lord owed his accomplishment to him. After brief amenities, the visitor anxiously inquired, in a tone mixed with agony with affection "Sir, after you pass away, who will succeed you?"

"Your Majesty," the prime minister humbly replied, in a feeble voice, "please keep away from Yee Ya,[8] Sue Dau,[9] Chan Ze-Wu,[10] and the baron Chi Fon.[11]" The master was greatly astonished because all of them were his most trusted assistants.

"Why Yee Ya? He is more than benevolent to me." questioned the lord. "Several years ago, to cure my ailment, he faithfully followed a doctor's prescription and used human flesh in the medicine. As a matter of fact, he killed and cooked his own baby and used its flesh to save my life. Why should I have doubts about him?"

"Please, his act is beyond my comprehension. Nobody in his right mind would not love his own son." the prime minister patiently explained. "He could ruthlessly butcher his own son for Your Majesty. Such atrocious behavior shows that he is both ambitious and cold-blooded. He lusts after fame and power even over the life of his own dear son. How can Your Majesty expect him to be faithful to you when you are in trouble?"

"How about Sue Dau?" the lord challenged. "He is truly devoted to me. To serve me in the palace, he voluntarily castrated himself. Should I suspect such a dedicated servant?"

"Of course Your Majesty must beware of him, even more than the first!" the ill minister exclaimed. "Before respecting and loving others, one must cherish oneself first. He crippled his body to attain Your Majesty's trust. He is unbelievable. He will do anything to reach his goals. I believe that to win a new master's confidence, he would sacrifice Your Majesty's life without any hesitation." The lord was silent for a few moments, laboriously searching his brain to figure out reliable points to support his coming statement. "Chan Ze-Wu is both a famous fortune-teller and knowledgeable medicine man." the lord impatiently remarked. "I have faith in him. He will never betray me."

"I am afraid that I have to disagree with Your Majesty." the prime minister sincerely responded. "Fate and illness are destined. No one can guarantee our fortune for us. By having too much confidence in this man, Your Majesty will indulgently grant him extra privileges. As a result, he will be spoiled and become arrogant and egotistical, wrongfully considering himself a living demi-god. He will become filled with wicked ambitions, and will gather wicked persons to assist him. Their collaboration will corrupt and eventually destroy the country."

"Damn it! According to your evaluation, I am surrounded by con men and swindlers!" Obviously infuriated, the lord continued. "How about baron Chi-Fon? We are close relatives. He treats me better than his father and has worked for me for over fifteen years. He didn't even leave my side to attend his own father's funeral ceremony. I trust him."

"I am sorry that I thought otherwise," the ailing host quietly answered. "People are bound by relationships. It is common sense that your blood relatives should be closer to you than those by marriage. We all love and respect our ancestors. It is one of the most essential human inclinations. The baron, who doesn't like his own father, couldn't be genuinely devout to a master, especially in a dreadful situation."

With surprise and displeasure, the lord, taking a long breath, pondered for a while and reluctantly agreed with the prime minister's logical estimation. Baffled and frustrated, he discontinued this gloomy conversation and left. Instead of designating a candidate to replace the dying prime minister, the lord unexpectedly discovered that all of his intimate aides and potential nominees were unreliable. What a shock!

In a few months, using various excuses, the lord demoted and relocated the men to other cities. Without their flattery and idolization, he felt lonely and depressed. After enduring that loneliness for three tedious years, one day, the lord murmured "How naive am I, listening to the ex-prime minister's dying babble? They made no error and were all so faithful to me. How could he, a dying, senile buffoon, have doubts about their loyalty? I shouldn't believe his far-fetched condemnation."

The lord then reestablished the men to their previous positions in the palace. They quickly regained his trust. Two years later, due to pampered living and lack of exercise, the aged lord, had a stroke which paralyzing half of his body. He was confined to bed all day. In that woeful condition, he couldn't even properly control his lips. Most of his ministers and servants were deeply distressed, except that handful of his trusted aides. They were exuberant about their good luck.

Conspiring with other unscrupulous officials, the fortune-teller spread rumors, indicating that their master would die on a certain date. The other two assistants, Yee Ya and Sue Dau, fabricated some absurd excuses and ordered workers to build thick, tall walls around the lord's bedroom. His communication with outside world was totally cut off.

Meticulously restricting human traffic fin and out of the palace, they used the name of their powerless master to issue orders to other high-ranking officials, and interfered with the state's policies for their personal benefit. No one knew what was happening to their lord, who was under tight surveillance.

To avoid a ruthless purge, the baron Chi-Fon, who belonged to another political faction, with over one thousand households, abandoned the emperor and fled to a neighboring country. Overhearing this incident, the lord moaned and cussed, in a remorseful tone. "I am really a damn fool! Why didn't I listen to my ex-prime minister's far-sighted advice?"

As an old saying goes, "Too much and not enough, both are improper." The true motivation of great sacrifice should be suspected and scrutinized.

Keep It Quiet

Warring States Period
475 B.C. to 221 B.C.

Is being too observant good or harmful? Comprehending your master's intention, should you execute it even before you are told? The following episode will illustrate one answer. It happened in the fifth century B.C.

A high-ranking government official named Tien Chen-Tze[12] and a regional general, Shyi Shih-Mi,[13] inspected a newly-built military fortress. Climbing a watchtower they stood and looked around, enjoying the panoramic scene. Their view was excellent except for a stand of tall trees that blocked a portion of the picturesque landscape. The trees belonged to the general. The general noticed that the official seemed to be dissatisfied that the trees were in the way, but no word was spoken of it.

Returning home, the general immediately assembled his male servants and zealously instructed them to chop down those bothersome trees as soon as possible. They promptly marched out with axes to do his bidding. But a few minutes later, with similar enthusiasm, he commanded them to ignore his first command and leave the trees standing. The puzzled servants grumbled to themselves and privately mocked their master for being indecisive. Later, one of the general's assistants curiously asked him about the incident.

"I thought my sharp observation would earn me some compliments." said the general. "However, after further contemplation I changed my mind. As an old maxim says, 'Knowing too much of another's private matters is a misfortune.' If I cut down those trees, the official, who was on a top-secret assignment and didn't want anybody to know it, would feel uncomfortable about the way I had read his reaction and, consequently, would become suspicious of me. He would keep a guarded eye on me and even wrongly classify me as a potential threat. My keen perception jeopardizes my neck. But if I deliberately play dumb, he will instruct me to remove those trees later on. He may even lightheartedly reprimand me for my thoughtlessness, but he will never doubt my allegiance. Then, my life is secured. That is the reason why I changed my mind."

A Fatal Disagreement

Southern Sung Dynasty
1127 A.D. to 1279 A.D.

In the early twelfth century A.D., northern China was conquered by barbarians. The capital was sacked and looted. In 1126 A.D., the emperor and his family were captured and taken northward to a faraway and frosty territory. One of the emperor's brothers, King Sung-Kao,[14] whose domain was undisturbed in the south, re-established the dynasty along the Yangtze river with himself as emperor.

In this new regime, government officials divided into two factions. One group wanted to recover the lost land, and the other preferred to negotiate with the enemy for peace, and give up the lost northern lands. If the enemy returned the captured emperor, the new emperor would be in a very difficult situation. He would be forced to either give up his current status or to initiate a civil war.

Not wanting to give up his newly-acquired power, the current emperor favored the latter faction. His prime minister, a shrewd and well-educated man, perceived his master's desire and openly advocated peace talks with the barbarians. However, most of the generals kept fighting the enemy, regardless of their emperor's plans. In the occupied territory, people didn't want to be governed by the uncivilized invaders. They zealously helped soldiers to expel the invaders.

In one bloody battle, the northern invaders were routed by the famous Chinese general Yueh Fei.[15] The barbarian prince Kin Wu-Shiu,[16] who was responsible for this military catastrophe, was dejected and seriously considered a complete withdrawal of his troops from China's former capital. This would greatly encourage other cities and towns to fight against their invaders. Consequently, the northern part of China would be recovered.

An advisor came to speak with the barbarian prince. "Your Highness doesn't need to evacuate your army at all. Your opponent Yueh Fei will be recalled soon. Without his leadership, his forces can't take over this city."

"Are you crazy? That's ridiculous!" With great astonishment, the prince, who was an experienced general, vigorously rebuked the advisor. "He is really a genius. With merely five hundred soldiers to start it with, he mustered and trained a few thousand civilians, and they completely defeated my one hundred thousand elite fighters. We have battled all our lives and never met such tough opponents. Our boys' confidence was shattered. They're afraid to engage in another skirmish. That son of bitch licked me hard this time. Furthermore, the city dwellers welcome Yueh Fei. They secretly sabotage our military depots. To tell you the truth, I'll be surprised if I return to our land with a third of my troops. How can you foresee my success?"

"Your Highness, although you are talented on battlefields, I am afraid that you are still naive about politics." This visitor shrewdly analyzed the situation. "In history, have you ever heard any heroes who outshone their masters and still kept their necks? Your opponent's fate was sealed by his exceptional accomplishment. Yueh Fei's success threatens the new emperor's position. Your opponent will be recalled."

Pondering for a long while, the prince suddenly burst into roars of laughter and agreed with this analysis. He ordered his troops to fortify the city. A few days later, Yueh Fei was summoned back to the new southern capital and slyly promoted to deputy defense minister, an honorary and powerless position. Due to his absence, major military engagements were discontinued. After months of negotiation, both countries signed a peace treaty, and the Southern Sung dynasty was firmly established. The new border was along the Yangtze river.

In addition, the crafty prime minister disliked Yueh Fei and was annoyed by his patriotic reputation. Some months later, the prime minister fabricated a far-fetched accusation and personally issued a warrant. The general was abruptly arrested, placed into a jail, put through a show trial, sentenced to death and quickly executed. At age 39, Yueh Fei was one of the youngest and ablest military leaders and strategists in Chinese history, but his life was cut short by the emperor's ambition.

Be aware when your goals are different from your master's, and your successes outshine his. Your life and career might be in jeopardy.

Practice Jogging

Western Han Dynasty
206 B.C to 25 A.D.

Perceiving an upcoming disaster is not enough to save yourself. You must also make a plan to deal with it. This interesting episode happened in the beginning of the first century A.D. The last few emperors were extremely young. Some of them were still babies. A notorious regent named Wong Mang[17] intended to murder the powerless child emperor Ju-Tzi-Ying[18] and snatch the crown for himself.

A fortune-teller named Zan Win-Gon[19] foresaw that the country would become a chaotic slaughterhouse. He ordered his family to shoulder two large baskets of rice, each one of them weighing fifty ponds, and practice jogging every day for hours. Giggling and cackling, neighbors were amused by their peddler-like appearances and exhausting exercise.

A few years later, the dynasty was overthrown. Several powerful lords and ambitious persons gathered their own armies and fought with one another for the throne. A series of battles devastated the country. Cities and farmlands were abandoned. Tens of thousands of people died of starvation and warfare. But among the few lucky survivors were the fortune-teller and his family, who not only saved their lives, but also carried enough grain to keep from starving.

A similar event occurred in the end of the Northern Sung dynasty in the early twelfth century A.D. A well-known prime minister, Tsay Gin,[20] hired a coach to teach his family members jogging. Although they didn't have an opportunity to use it, I think it was for the same reason.

Besides having a keen observation, one must always be prepared. Don't waste time naively wondering whether a misfortune will come or not. It is irrelevant. The real point is, are you ready if it does come?

Strange Construction
Tang Dynasty
618 A.D. to 907 A.D.

During the end of the Tang dynasty, a powerful warlord named Zou Win[21] was openly hostile towards the loyal governor Lee Ker-Yuon[22] and the vulnerable Emperor Tang-Chao.[23] Zou Win wanted to set himself up as emperor.

In a certain temple, a new pagoda was under construction. The old monk in charge ordered workers to store dry goods between the walls. Furthermore, he deliberately purchased extra wooden columns that were unnecessary to support the ceiling. Observing this peculiar behavior, most of the other monks sneered at him behind his back and figured he was getting weak in the head.

A few months after the pagoda was finished, a civil war broke out. Soldiers and rebels were everywhere. Merchants discontinued their trades. Farmers dared not attend their rice fields. Cities were sacked and towns burned. Many people perished in this calamity. Then winter came. Due to the shortage of food, a grain of rice was worth an equal-sized pearl. Nobody wanted to sell their scarce farm products. Many rich people, holding costly but useless jewelry, died of starvation.

During the chaos, the monk directed his apprentices to recover the hidden dry goods and tear down the excess pillars for firewood. The monks were saved from starvation and from the cold. They admired the old monk for his farsightedness and wisdom.

Any News?

Ming Dynasty
1368 A.D. to 1644 A.D.

In the old days, imperial China was governed by a string of dynasties. The periods between dynasties were often times of political and economic chaos. Many people would perish in man-made disasters. And after a new dynasty was established, many more people would be slaughtered by suspicious emperors looking to secure their new position. The following episode happened in the late fourteenth century A.D.

After years of battles, the barbarian-ruled Yuan dynasty, 1206 A.D. to 1368 A.D., was overthrown. Since the Yuan dynasty's capital was in Peking, where most of the battles took place, much of the damage was confined to Northern China. Cities had been sacked and towns ruined. Mansions were leveled and buildings burned to the ground. Many people, suddenly homeless, suffered hunger and poverty.

However, Southern China, had been less affected, especially the prosperous Southern Kiangsu area, located south of the Yangtze river and near the eastern coast. The lands were very productive and the people affluent. Local citizens benefited from the region's well-cultivated rice fields and prosperous silk trade, and had enjoyed a relatively undisturbed lifestyle for generations.

A rich merchant named Wan Er,[24] visited one of his friends, who recently returned from the new capital city, Nanking. Due to the bloody transfer of the dynasty, the merchants were very concerned about politics. What was the attitude of the new government towards wealthy families?

Wan Er's friend told him that he overheard an interesting anecdote. The new emperor Ming-Tai[25] wrote a poem to complain about his position. It read: "Before any of my subordinates wake up, I must be ready to receive them. After they are deeply sleep, I still have to review their reports for hours. What a dreadful and monotonous task! If I had a choice now, I would rather be a merchant in the Southern Kiangsu area. They snore till noon everyday."

"This is a very bad omen." said Wan Er. "Our Majesty is jealous of our prosperity. I have a hunch that jealousy will turn to persecution someday."

He returned home and summoned all of his servants for instructions. He immediately put up all of his properties for sale and liquidated other assets. Then he purchased two huge commercial ships. In a few weeks, he dismissed most of his servants and meticulously directed a few faithful assistants to take care of his remaining businesses. Then, with all his close family members and wealth on board, he sailed out of the country.

In less than two years, the new emperor began a cruel political oppression. He deliberately targeted prosperous families in Southern China. With far-fetched indications of treason or conspiracy, most of the wealthy merchants, one after the other, were arrested, tortured, prosecuted and imprisoned or executed. All their land and personal property was confiscated, and family members were sold as slaves or banished from their mansions and forced to became beggars.

CHAPTER SIX

Reckon and Calculate

Not a Real Friend

A person with wealth and fame will certainly have many friends and acquaintances. However, deprived of those two possessions, that person may suddenly find that those cordial friends have become cold-blooded enemies. But how to tell? This episode happened in the late fifth century B.C.

After a severe power struggle, a defeated official named Gin Win-Tzy[1] fled his country, seeking sanctuary in other realms. As his carriages passed a small city, one of his assistants kindly suggested, "Your Highness, the mayor here was your vassal once. Why don't we take a break here?"

"Ha! He is a crook and will sell me out to advance his political career." the master thunderously shouted over the noise of the carriage. "I used to love music and he gave me a valuable flute. I liked jewelry and he gave me costly jades. He always tried to flatter me, and that is the reason why I avoid him. He is a sycophant, and his only loyalty is to himself. Now that I'm a wanted man, my only value to him is the price on my head. We must pass this city at once."

The minister's own carriage sped past the city. However, two of his other coaches were observed, captured, and sent back to his opponents for a reward.

Never be deceived by smiling faces and cordial attitudes. You must always contemplate the true reasons behind graciousness.

Befriend Whom?

During the Spring and Autumn period, China was unfortunately in disarray. A senior eunuch named Miow Shan,[2] who once was the King's favorite servant, violated the law and planned to escape to a neighboring country. His friend Lin Shan-Lu[3] asked, "Where did you get such an idea? Why do you think you will be safe there?"

"I once accompanied our king to a peace conference held there," the eunuch explained. "At the welcoming party, their King privately swore to me that he and I would be like brothers. That's why I want to seek shelter there. I believe he is a man of honor and will save my life."

"Don't be naive! Let us analyze the situation." With a dry smile, the friend said "Our country is very strong. When you went there, you were the assistant with the most influence on our King. Who wouldn't flatter you? They were using you to make a good impression on our master. You were an intermediary for them. They are afraid of our country and wanted to get along with our ruler, not with you, a mere servant. If you solicit their help, they'll immediately arrest you and send you back to please our master. Your escape will fail."

The eunuch realized his friend was correct. With a piteous wail he cried "Then what should I do?"

"Immediately go see our King, admit your wrongdoing, and beg for mercy. Recalling your past performance, he might spare your life." The eunuch considered this a while and agreed to do so.

Two Prime Ministers

Tang Dynasty
618 A.D. to 907 A.D.

In the old days, high-ranking officials often belonged to different political factions. To uphold their own prominence, they severely competed with one another to win the ruler's trust. As a part of this feud, when the leader of a faction died, his reputation would most likely be smeared by opposing factions and his offspring might be put to death. How could a minister protect his reputation and ensure the safety of his family? With a clever plot, of course. This amusing episode happened in the early Tang dynasty.

Two prime ministers, Yau Czon[4] and Jang Shou,[5] were famous for their shrewdness. However, they disliked each other. One day, Prime Minster Yau Czon fell into serious illness. On his deathbed, he carefully instructed his sons to follow a plan.

"My colleague, Prime Minister Jang Shuo,[6] is both the most educated scholar in our government and the most influential official in our country. Everybody knows that we detest each other and have competed against each other for years. Once I die, I am sure he would like nothing better than to besmirch my reputation and eliminate my family."

"But how can we protect your reputation and save our lives?" asked the sons nervously.

"Jang Shou loves to collect rare and expensive treasures." answered the old man. "After I pass away, he, out of politeness, will visit our family. You must display all of my most valuable possessions next to my coffin. If he doesn't pay any attention to them, your fates are sealed. He will fabricate excuses and persecute you all. But if he scrutinizes them, you must give them all to him and, as is tradition, beseech him to write a eulogy to commemorate me. Since I am no longer a threat to his ambitions, and because of the treasures, he will be more than happy to write many glowing words about my character.

"After he finishes this eulogy, immediately make a copy. Hire a renowned sculptor to carve it on my tombstone and quickly send the original to Our Majesty for approval. My colleague is smart, but rather slow-witted when it comes to analyzing a situation. A few days later, he will come to ask for that paper back. You should politely tell him that article is already in the imperial palace for a review and show him the engraved tombstone."

Everything occurred as the dying minister predicted. In the eulogy, this colleague, who was very pleased to receive the valuables for free, greatly complimented the deceased prime minister and overlooked the fact that he was a political opponent.

Two days later, he anxiously came to request that eulogy back to make some 'minor corrections,' and was informed according to the instructions. "Damn it!" he cursed. "Yau Czon outwitted me one last time." With his political opponent's 'endorsement,' the deceased prime minister and his family members were safe from any prosecution.

One Man Show

How to deal with a potential rebellion? You may dispatch a larger number of soldiers to repress them militarily. However, since their treason is not indisputable and your maneuver is costly and time-consuming, you should seriously consider other alternatives. There was a similar event happened in the late eighth century A.D.

Jang Chuan, the commander of a remote province was poisoned by his deputy commander, Dachi Bau-Huei,[7] who made up an excuse for this untimely death and asked the central government to promote him to that position.

But a loyal servant who had heard of the plot fled to the capital and informed the authorities about this murder. As a result, all the officials in the capital knew of this tragedy. The emperor Tang-Teh[8] was infuriated and appointed a commissioner named Lee Mi[9] to handle this case. He intended to muster many well-trained imperial guards to escort him.

"No, Your Majesty," the commissioner confidently remarked, "the soldiers in that garrison are innocent. They didn't know this conspiracy at all. Only the deputy commander has to be punished. If I march there in force, that sly deputy might start a war. Then we would need at least six months and over ten thousands soldiers to conquer that city. I think I can deal with this situation personally." Impressed by the commissioner's confidence, the emperor agreed with his analysis. The commissioner then spread a rumor that due to famine in the rural areas, the government assigned him to deliver hundreds of tons of rice for the suffering people. Furthermore, he was secretly appointed to evaluate the potential commander's credibility and ability. Overhearing this, the deputy commander felt pleased.

After days of travel, the commissioner arrived on the outskirts of the city, with only a few well-trained bodyguards disguised as servants. It was a custom for the regional commander to personally welcome an official from the capital. The deputy, protected by many armed soldiers, cautiously received him. In the public, the commissioner highly praised the man for governing the garrison so well after the commander's premature death.

Seeing the commissioner's small number of attendants, Dachi Bau-Huei relaxed and cheerfully ushered them to the garrison. Lee Mi was conducted to the military headquarters, where he would stay during his visit. That night, an unknown a visitor wanted to report a 'top secret' message to the commissioner, but he flatly refused to admit him. This event was known by the host, who was more than pleased and trusted this guest even more.

While the commissioner was there, he spent all his time studying data and charts relating to the famine. Some local servants privately hinted about the commander's suspicious death. The commissioner immediately dismissed them for being trouble-making rumor mongers.

Later, at a gathering, in front of a few thousand soldiers, the commissioner confidently explained: "Gentlemen, since arriving here, I have heard many groundless rumors about your deputy commander. But, I am not a censor. Please remember this. I am here to deliver the rice for the needy, nothing else. Currently, you don't have a commander yet, so it is understandable that vicious gossip prevails. But I don't want to hear it anymore."

The next day, the local guards who had been assigned to 'guard' the visitor's residence were removed; so were many plainclothes spies. Believing that his plot had been undetected, the deputy commander joyfully called on the commissioner. At first, they chatted cordially. After a while, the commissioner courteously requested that the deputy commander remove all of his guards, so that they could speak privately. This order was carried out immediately, and the two men were left alone in the commissioner's chambers.

The deputy commander smiled, believing this to be the moment when his promotion would be granted. But the commissioner revealed his true purpose. "I know you murdered your commander and I am here to remove you. The whole house is under my loyal bodyguards' control. I could kill you this instant if I desired. However, I am going to spare your life, but not because of your virtue or talent. I simply don't want our government to give a wrong impression to the people. Sign this paper now and I will guarantee the safety of you and your family. You must leave this city."

Dumfounded and frightened, the deputy commander noticed a few 'servants' coming out from behind a long curtain. Trembling and pale-faced, he signed the paper and surrendered all his authority to the commissioner. The host then ordered his bodyguards to accompany this deputy and his family out of the city under the cover of night. Next morning he called an urgent military conference and disclosed his real identity. He then announced that their deputy commander had voluntarily 'resigned' himself, and suggested all the attending generals elect a temporary leader among themselves, which was happily carried out. A senior general was properly selected.

In a few days, all the other conspirators, mostly mid-level officers, were arrested and charged with treason. Due to the commissioner's insistence, they were pardoned by the emperor and relocated to other garrisons. The whole political conspiracy was quietly and cleverly resolved by the commissioner's shrewdness and boldness.

Build a Military Fortress

Northern Chou Dynasty
557 A.D. to 581 A.D.

In the middle of the sixth century A.D., a senior general named Woei Shiaw-Kuan[10] wanted to build a military fortress on a strategically important site near the border. He assembled one hundred thousand workers and one hundred soldiers, and assigned his aide Yau Yueh[11] to supervise this construction.

Since that location was close to their belligerent enemy, an attack was very likely. Without well-equipped and heavily armed troops to protect the workers, the whole project was vulnerable. The aide was worried about security, and courteously suggested that his superior increase the number of the soldiers.

"Don't worry about that," the general confidently explained. "I already meticulously calculated. That is the reason why I assembled so many people. With such plentiful manpower, we can build his castle in ten days. If we start building today, our hostile neighbor won't notice until tomorrow. Then it would take at least two days for them to assemble an army. Furthermore, they have to discuss all the pros and cons of initiating such aggressive military action, which will cost them another three to four days. After they decided to attack us, their infantrymen have to march a full two days to reach the construction site. By then, our castle is already finished!"

In addition to such a detailed calculation, the general took other precautions as well. On the day construction began, the general secretly ordered his captains at other corners of the border to burn dried hay. This drew the enemy's attention to those remote outposts, and enemy soldiers were transported to away from the construction site. They wrongfully thought that their garrisons would be under attack and focused their attention on these distractions. In ten days, the castle was duly completed and the enemy didn't notice until it was too late.

Leave It to Others

Eastern Han Dynasty
25 A.D. to 220 A.D.

There is an old saying, "Never chase after an escaped enemy." After winning a decisive battle, you don't need to finish the job yourself. Others will do it for you. It is not to your best advantage to push the defeated too far. They will be eliminated by others who want to demonstrate their fidelity to you. The following story illustrates this old saying.

In 200 A.D. China was unfortunately in a period of disunity. It was a time of chaos and disorder. Warlords fought fiercely with one another for domination. Emperor Han-Hsien,[12] was being held as a hostage by a shrewd prime minister named Tsaur Tsau,[13] who was too cunning to crown himself. The prime minister's forces had recently won a decisive battle over the most powerful warlord, Yuan Shau.[14]

The warlord's two sons, with a few thousand faithful bodyguards, fled the region and sought political asylum from governor Gonsun Kan,[15] whose domain was a remote and less cultivated north-eastern territory. Most of the prime minister's assistants urged him to hunt down and annihilate the fugitives, and the governor who was harboring them.

"Either you are joking," chided the prime minister, "or you don't understand human nature at all. Why should we waste another ounce of energy chasing those sons when others will be more than happy to do it for us? That governor used to cooperate with the warlord because their territories adjoined. But now that I have conquered the warlord and taken his territory, our borders touch. The governor is afraid that I might continue my offensive—against him! He will chop those fugitives' heads off without hesitation and courteously deliver them to my doorstep to display his allegiance to me."

Though skeptical, nobody dared to argue with their superior. However, most of them considered this reasoning to be a far-fetched excuse for his inactivity. But a few months later, the heads were conveyed to the capital. All the aids were astonished. With great curiosity they asked him about this amazing prophecy.

"It's very simple. You simply have to understand one of human nature's fundamental inclinations; to flirt with the strong and trample the doomed. We are now the great regional power. To maintain his own realm, the governor must demonstrate his 'loyalty' to me. Consequently, that pair of heads was the cheapest and most practical way to do so."

Be Humble

Three Kingdoms Period
220 A.D. to 265 A.D.

After achieving some measure of success, a foolish person may become arrogant. His egotistical attitude will discourage and disgust his true friends, who will forsake him. Sycophants will replace his friends. Eventually, he will be ruined by his own arrogance. As an old saying goes, "No matter how intelligent you are, you could always find out someone who is smarter than you are." Confucius once lectured, "In a group of three persons, they must have something that is worthwhile for me to learn." The lesson is to be humble. There is always something that you can learn. Here is a conversation that illustrates this principle.

In the middle of the third century A.D., during the chaotic Three Kingdoms period, there was a statesman named Lu Shiun[16] who was famous for his shrewdness and far-sightedness. One day this statesman was chatting with Zuger Keh,[17] an intimate friend.

"To keep away from trouble, you must be humble all the time," Lu Shiun sincerely advised. "I honestly respect and learn from the person who is more intelligent than me. I do my best to assist those who are less clever than me. Unfortunately, according to my observation, you do otherwise. You alienate yourself from the former and sneer at the later. Consequently, intelligent people won't give you their valuable advice, and others will despise you. You will have many opponents and not one single genuine compatriot. In the long run, you will be in big trouble."

Zuger Keh was dumbfounded by his host's frankness. He refused to listen to this perceptive suggestion and angrily left. A few years later, he was mercilessly slaughtered in a political struggle.

Humbleness is the best protection to shield yourself against jealousy and resentment. Actively assisting others will win appreciation and future support. Mastering those two manners will bring you many faithful friends.

CHAPTER 7

Analyze the Doubtful

Try It On You

Northern Sung Dynasty, 960 A.D. to 1127 A.D.

Flattering the powerful is a common practice, especially in political situations. The upright are disgusted by this kind of behavior. How to correct it? An amusing episode from the Northern Sung dynasty offers this suggestion.

General Tsiao Ker-Min[1] was relocated to a border city. One day a local chieftain, in order to butter up the new general, visited him and gave him a small bottle of ointment. He zealously boasted that this medicine could rapidly cure any wound or cut caused by arrows.

"If Your Highness doesn't believe it," he proudly announced, "you could test it on a chicken or a dog."

"Are you joking?" cried the general, who took offense at the chieftain's tone. "Why waste such magic medicine on an animal? On the battlefield, we heal people's wounds, not chickens' or dogs'. I have a better idea. I think I'll try it on you!"

The chieftain's proud smirk vanished and he began to tremble and shiver. The general promptly fetched an arrow, stabbed it into the visitor's thigh, and then applied the ointment over the cut. The hapless chieftain fainted and had to be carried home, where he stayed in bed for several weeks. Overhearing this, other chieftains were astonished and dared not to try flattery on this new general.

A Phony Conspiracy

Western Han Dynasty
206 B.C. to 25 A.D.

In the old days, an emperor had absolute power. When he was young and unsophisticated, wicked ministers would often would fabricate false evidence and maliciously accuse their political opponents. As a saying says, "Even if you could prove your innocence, your credibility would be greatly smeared." A similar plot happened in the middle of the first century B.C.

The newly-enthroned child emperor Han-Chao[2], one day received an urgent letter from his elder brother, King Yan,[3] revealing that the prime minister Huoh Gwan[4] had inspected several imperial guard barracks and intended to start a coup. After pondering the matter for awhile, the emperor quietly pocketed the letter and made no comment.

Overhearing the accusation, the prime minister was terrified and dared not to enter the palace. In that era, for less serious accusations, many dedicated ministers were arrested and executed without a proper investigation.

Not seeing the prime minister among other high-ranking officials during a routine conference, the emperor abruptly dispatched a eunuch to summon him. With great uneasiness, the prime minister hesitantly went to meet his master. In the court he humbly took off his hat, a gesture of resignation, and zealously defended himself.

"Sir, I believe your innocence. You don't need to say another word for yourself. I knew this letter is fake." The emperor, then age fourteen, gently soothed the older man. The prime minister was astonished and courteously asked him about the reason.

"It is very simple. With some common sense and mathematics, you could immediately detect its falsehood." the observant ruler confidently explained. "Your inspection of the imperial guards in my brother the king's territory occurred less than ten days ago. Nobody knew of it beforehand. The distance between our capital city and the king's domain takes more than a week to travel one-way. There is no way anyone could know of your inspection, write this letter, and deliver it to me so soon. I think the crook who constructed this letter to ruin your reputation is still in the city, and I have already appointed my aides to investigate this matter."

All the commissioners were amazed, and highly respected the young emperor for his keen observation. Overhearing this news, the person who forged that letter was frightened and abruptly fled from the city at night.

Obtain the Evidence   *Northern Sung Dynasty*
960 A.D. to 1127 A.D.

In traditional Chinese imperial society, the single most difficult and delicate post was probably that of an emperor's heir. This heir often would become the target of various political factions or jealous princes. On the other hand, the heir or his supporters might start a palace coup or civil war to overthrow the present emperor. If an overthrow plot was discovered, how might you uncover evidence while not alerting the plotters? This interesting scenario was played out in the late tenth century A.D.

A rumor spread that the emperor's heir, Chau Yuan-Jo,[5] intended to initiate a palace coup d'etat against the present ruler. From a logical viewpoint this allegation was absurd because the heir, with patience, could assume his father's crown in a few years. However, the heir was both cruel and short-tempered and didn't want to wait.

Emperor Sung-Tai Tsung,[6] took counsel with a commissioner named Kwo Joen,[7] who was famous for his wisdom.

"Your Majesty, this is a very serious accusation," he shrewdly calculated. "We need solid evidence to convict your heir. Otherwise, his followers will have an excuse to disturb the tranquillity of the dynasty and even start a civil war."

"If we need evidence then I will order his palace to be searched. I'll send soldiers right away." said the emperor.

"Your Majesty, a daylight house-search will cause unnecessary disturbance and would certainly alert them of our suspicions." Hearing this, the ruler was deeply annoyed.

"However," continued the commissioner, "we could trick him out of his mansion. Then, we will have plenty of time to search every inch of that place. Your Majesty could give him the honor of supervising the upcoming holiday. During his absence, our men can comb his house. If he did violate the laws, any judge will be more than capable to take care of him." Beaming a smile, the emperor agreed.

On the designated date, the heir proudly went to direct that famous festival, accompanied by all of his trusted aides and many bodyguards. Meanwhile, a group of elite imperial guards brought a search warrant to the heir's mansion. They meticulously examined the prince's estate and discovered many unlawful possessions and conspiratorial plans, which they turned over to their master.

When the prince returned from the holiday, the emperor showed him the evidence he'd found. The prince was astonished. He admitted his wrongdoing and begged for mercy, but the emperor dismissed him on the spot. The next morning, the prince's violations, confession, and verdict were disclosed to the public in great detail. Soon everyone knew that the traitorous heir had been removed.

The ministers and palace officials praised the emperor for his wisdom in handling the situation. Neither a civil war nor an imperial coup materialized. Even the heir's most fanatic supporters were quiet and inactive. Without popular support, they dared not originate a fruitless riot that would accomplish nothing but jeopardize their own necks.

Facts are the most effective and convincing language when spoken in the period of doubt and crisis. As long as you can properly present them, you will not only win over your people but also your ferocious opponents.

The River Patron

Warring States Period
475 B.C. to 221 B.C.

Superstitions are ways for people to rationalize the unknown. In the old days people believed everything had patrons. To promote general welfare, the people routinely worshipped those patrons and offered up expensive dishes and popular dramas. Their behavior was understandable. However, those beliefs were often manipulated by the wicked for their own gain. This amusing event happened in the Warring States period.

Once, a newly appointed mayor named Shiman Bau[8] arrived at his domain and cordially invited some old men to his office. He courteously asked for their suggestions regarding local affairs.

"Sir, there is one thing that is especially bothering us." an old man anxiously uttered. "Every year, the city government requires us to pay a special tax for the marriage of the river patron. Many thousands of dollars are collected, yet they spend less than ten percent of the money on that strange practice. The rest is divided among several officials and a few witches. Worse than that, a few months before the ceremony, they seize several beautiful girls as 'brides' for the river patron. On the day of the 'wedding,' those miserable brides are dressed up and placed on a wooden bed in the river. They sink to the bottom and never appear again. Furthermore, those witches threaten us, saying that if we don't respect this custom, the river patron will get angry and the river will overflow, and many people will drown many farms will be destroyed. The local officials are on the side of the witches, protecting them. What can we do?"

"What an interesting custom." said the mayor. "I am fascinated. I would like to see it myself. Next time, please inform me. I will personally attend the ceremony."

The old men were surprised. After chatting about some matters of trivial importance, the mayor cheerfully ushered them out of his office. The old men were more confused than before. They didn't know whether they should praise or curse this mayor, who seemed so sincere about listening to their complaints but then offered no solutions, nor even a verbal appeasement. Eventually they agreed that this new mayor wanted a share of the profits and would do nothing to stop the custom.

A few months later the mayor was invited as a guest of honor to the river patron festival. He joyfully accepted and duly arrived. Several thousand curious people crowded the riverside. Many government officials were also in attendance.

Observing a peculiarly-dressed witch, who was surrounded by a handful of assistants, the mayor mannerly bowed to her and then casually examined the frightened brides.

After a brief inspection he turned and shouted at the witch in a disgusted voice. "Are you out of your mind? You must be joking. Where are your eyes? Open them up! Can't you see that these girls are ugly? Offering such obnoxious louts will irritate our mighty river patron! We have to delay this ceremony for a few days until we can locate a few suitable beauties. We can't afford to lose face." Never hearing this kind of stern criticism before, everyone was startled and speechless. Turning his head and glaring menacingly, the mayor asked the witch, who was dumbstruck with confusion, to notify the patron of the delay.

Immediately the mayor's bodyguards seized the witch and placed her on the bed in the river, which promptly sank.

The mayor waited for several minutes, and then declared "What a lucky lady! The patron treats her well. She must be drunk and have lost her direction. We need someone to look for her." He then ordered his guards to select one of the witch's senior aids and drop her into the river.

After four similar treatments the mayor declared "Well! What is wrong with them? Why don't they come back? Must be a bunch of irresponsible and unreliable boozers. Maybe a man could do the job better." He then directed his muscular servants to throw a few government officials into the water. After their heads went under for the last time, the mayor reproachfully glared at the other involved officials, who were so frightened that they immediately knelt and pleaded for mercy. With an icy smile, he contemptuously scrutinized them and then calmly left.

From that day on, nobody dared to mention the ceremony again, and the tax was conveniently forgotten. The local citizens were exhilarated by the new mayor's shrewd behavior, and his subordinates never dared to monkey around with their clever master.

Buddha's Tooth
Later Tang Dynasty
923 A.D. to 936 A.D.

In the old days, people frequently worshipped sacred objects. Swindlers often took advantage of peoples' faith, claiming to be in possession of a holy bone or two. Using it, they could easily accumulate a fortune. This amusing event happened in the early tenth century A.D.

A monk visited the imperial palace and proudly proclaimed to have the tooth of Buddha. He claimed that he had been in Western territory for years, and was a well-cultivated and religious hermit. In the next routine royal conference, the emperor L. Tang-Min[9] presented that divine tooth, placed in the middle of a decorated jewel box and guarded by two servants, to the ministers. Observing it, most of the ministers immediately gave their compliments and favorable remarks.

When this divine item was passed to a middle-level official named Chau Fon,[10] he stepped forward and courteously said "How lucky our dynasty is to have such a priceless treasure. By the way, according to a well-known legend, Buddha's tooth is indestructible. If I may suggest, Your Majesty could test it."

The emperor agreed and ordered an eunuch to hammer the tooth with the back of an ax. It was crushed into powder by the very first strike. All the observers were dumbfounded. They immediately realized that they had been fooled. The fortune-seeking monk was put in jail. From that day on, nobody dared to peddle false relics to the palace in exchange for a government position or a handsome reward.

The same deceptions occurred in the Ming dynasty. Once, checking the imperial warehouse's inventory, officials were astonished to find over one ton of 'holy' teeth, bones, and skulls. It indicated that there were many unscrupulous job-seekers who contributed a bone and obtained a position from the government. They were the unforgivable sinners of Buddhism.

A Gold-Covered Icon

Ming Dynasty
1368 A.D. to 1644 A.D.

How to deal with superstition? This interesting story happened during the Ming dynasty. In South-Western China, there was a certain area of the country that believed in ghosts and spirits. In the early sixteenth century, A.D., a censor named Lin Jiun[11] once traveled through a city and saw many persons assembled around a temple. Stopping by, he was surprised to see that they were anxiously spreading pure gold, in powder form, all over a large wooden statue of a Buddha.

Infuriated by their absurd behavior, he sternly ordered his bodyguards to seize that glittering statue, intending to burn it down. As he was instructing other servants to fetch dried branches, he was interrupted by an old man.

"Please, Your Highness, spare our lives. Don't give us a hard time." he pleaded, tears rolling down from his cheeks. "If you destroy our icon, the almighty will be mad and curse us all. A deadly hail will drop from the heavens. Our farm lands will be ruined!"

"Nonsense," the official harshly rebuked, and quickly ordered his men to build a bonfire, which was complete in a few moments. Some of his servants laboriously heaved the gold-covered statue onto fire.

The censor signaled them to halt. Then he raised his eyes to the sky and loudly announced "I take full responsibility for destroying this icon. If there is to be any curse from heaven, I want it to fall on me! Send me a sign at this very moment or I will toss this icon to the fire without further delay."

All the observers were astonished. They were terrified that a sudden lightning bolt meant for the blasphemous censor might strike them by mistake. Looking at one another with amazement, they dared not to say a word. After a few minutes of deadly silence, marked only by a gentle wind and that caressed everyone's foreheads, nothing unusual happened. The censor directed his bodyguards to throw this statue into the fire.

"Oh!" gasped the onlookers as their icon caught fire and burned fiercely. It was totally destroyed in minutes.

Hours later, the fire was out and the ashes had cooled. The censor ordered his servants to examine the site. After a meticulous search, they collected a few hundred ounces of gold, which was duly delivered to the local authority.

Deal with superstition on the spot. You can both prove its falsehood and eliminate others' skepticism.

Flail Oneself
Southern Sung Dynasty
1127 A.D. to 1279 A.D.

If you don't like a peculiar custom, how should you, as a local authority, react? Of course, you could issue an ordinance to prohibit it. However, your high-handed behavior would unsuitably earn you notoriety. If you do nothing to oppress it, you will be condemned by your own self-consciousness for the inactivity. Then, how can you both uphold your reputation and satisfy your consciousness?

This interesting event happened during the Southern Sung dynasty. In a rural area, as a local tradition, a sinner would flail himself in public to make up for some misconduct.

Hwan Jan,[12] the newly-appointed mayor to the province, didn't like this tradition and wanted it to stop. But he also didn't want to irritate the local people by banning their traditions, which would only cause resentment and future difficulties. By chance one afternoon he observed a person in the crowded public square gently and nervously lashing himself. The mayor suddenly realized an opportunity. He ordered his bodyguards to detain that person, and then demanded that the man confess his violation.

"Sir, I am not doing any wrong. Why do you harass me?" the man protested.

"Don't wisecrack with me!" the mayor sneered. "You must have committed some crime. Otherwise, you would not be flailing yourself in public, trying to appeal to the Almighty to forgive you. But I am afraid the Almighty hasn't noticed yet. Let me assist you to ensure your success."

He immediately commanded his guards to throw the man to the ground and severely beat his buttocks with thick rods. After suffering twenty solid strikes, a common punishment for a misdemeanor, the man was released. Moaning and groaning, he limped away. All the bystanders were astonished. They quickly spread the news of this event to every corner of the city. In hours, everybody knew it. From that day on, nobody dared to flail himself in the public again. This strange custom was eliminated.

What a clever mayor! His reason was perfectly logical and nobody dared to argue with him. Furthermore, his behavior could even be interpreted as an assistance, although it was not a pleasant one. The mayor's example would certainly discourage others to practice that custom for fear of receiving his vigorous 'assistance.' Without a written order, that strange tradition was exterminated.

CHAPTER EIGHT

Orchestrate the Complexes

Learn Archery

Northern Sung Dynasty
960 A.D. to 1127 A.D.

How do you motivate your people? For educated persons, fame and position could inspire them. On the other hand, for the common majority, money is still the single most efficient stimulus. This interesting story happened in the eleventh century A.D.

A general named Chorng Shyh-Herng[1] was assigned to a far-off and dangerous border city near the hostile northern barbarians. The soldiers stationed there were both ill-fed and badly-trained. Local trade was poor. Peddlers didn't want to risk their lives traveling there for only meager profits. To boost the local economy, the new commander eliminated some archaic ordinances and provided government loans at a low interest rate to merchants who were willing to stay for a year or more. Neighboring city residents were thrilled. They cheerfully relocated themselves to the outskirts of the garrison. After receiving the money, they immediately undertook their own small businesses. Trade posts and grocery stores were rapidly built. Peddlers began to bring their wares. But besides the economy, the general was also concerned about regional defense. To ask the central government to reinforce this remote outpost was impractical. They had to depend on themselves. So after the local commerce was stabilized, the general taught his assistants and clerks how to shoot with a bow and arrow. He made regulations that everyone, including monks, Daoists, women, and teenagers must be familiar with archery. Inspiring them to practice, he erected targets along the streets, and used a silver coin as a bull's eye. Under the watchful eyes of local soldiers, whoever placed an arrow in the hole of the coin could keep it as a reward. Furthermore, he demanded that petty lawbreakers shoot at targets. Their punishments were decided by their score—the worse the score, the more unpleasant. After years of encouragement, the city became famous for its people's skillful archery, and no barbarian tribes dared to invade.

As an old saying goes, "You must not waste your time on worrying about whether your enemy will or will not attack you. You must maximize your limited resources and be ready for the worst. As a result, your enemy dares not offend you." Be fully prepared. You are the only savior of your own future.

Follow the Right Route

Ming Dynasty
1368 A.D. to 1644 A.D.

In the old days, as a display of good will, neighboring countries would send their representatives to deliver gifts to China. However, if the representatives changed their travel route, how should China react? The most optimistic assumption was that they followed the wrong directions by mistake. On the other hand, the worst hypothesis was that they intended to survey the land for their next invasion. This was a touchy issue too small to make a formal, diplomatic complaint out of, but too big to be overlooked. If you were the Chinese emperor, what would your reaction be? A similar episode happened in the late fifteen century A.D.

As a diplomatic custom, northern barbarian tribes would routinely send some delegates, on a specific route, to visit the capital of China. After exchanging presents with Chinese government officials, they would be generously entertained. Once however, due to unknown reasons, the representatives came by a different route.

Informed by local officials of this unusual development, Emperor Ming-Hsien[2] was irritated and only reluctantly agreed to receive them. Their conversation was brief and rigid. After the visitors withdrew themselves from the imperial palace, Yau Kwei,[3] the minister for barbarian affairs, strongly suggested to his master that all the grandiose receptions and banquets, which were standard for welcoming those honorable guests, should be canceled. His advice was approved.

The delegates were treated as ordinary visitors without any privileges at all. They were enraged and protested to the appropriate department.

"Of course we would greet you properly," the minister answered, "if you followed the correct diplomatic route. But you did not, which is a violation. You have become lawbreakers and automatically forfeit your respectable status. Furthermore, to tell you the truth, we now doubt whether your credentials are genuine or not because of your odd behavior. That is the reason why we have to treat you as common foreigners rather than diplomatic personnel." Showing obvious dissatisfaction, the representatives acquiesced and accepted their treatment with silence.

China's behavior may seem fussy from a contemporary viewpoint. However, it made perfect sense at the time. The Northern barbarians were frequently at war with China, so yielding a needless inch could jeopardize national security. If the emperor treated the delegates as cordially as before, they might use this precedent from then on to select their own routes. They could send military experts, with diplomatic passports, to survey the land in preparation for a large-scale attack. Thus, the emperor's demand for rigid adherence to established routes was in the best interest of the nation.

Consul With the Old

Ming Dynasty
1368 A.D. to 1644 A.D.

In the Oriental societies, people respect the old. Why? Because, generally, they have a great deal of experience on which to draw. This interesting story happened in sixteenth century A.D.

A county mayor named Jo Zen,[4] who was famous for his competence, frequently sailed a small boat around his domain. One day he saw an old farmer, and decided to invite him to his home. They cordially exchanged opinions about local affairs. At night, he shared his bed with this shabbily-dressed guest. From the conversation, the mayor learned about the local citizens' opinions toward his policies. He invited the old man to his home many times, and often modified his legislation according to their discussions. During the mayor's eighteen years of leadership, he legislated many favorable rules and ordinances. The local people treated him almost like one of their own parents.

The Proper Price of Rice

Northern Sung Dynasty
960 A.D. to 1127 A.D.

Generally speaking, the free market system is the most efficient method for coping with food shortages. In the old days, when an area of the country suffered famine, local authorities often set a ceiling on the price of food, prohibiting merchants from earning excessive profits. But that wasn't the best way, as a county mayor proved in the middle of the eleventh century A.D.

Some parts of Southern China were suffering through a serious drought and a plague of locust. Thousands of people perished because of lack of food. Taking advantage of the situation, many speculators jacked up the price of rice and smuggled it there from afar. Most of the regional governors sternly prohibited this price increase, and enacted tough laws to oppose it. As a result, the unlawful transportation was discontinued, but the supply of grain coming into the area dropped, and the food shortage became worse.

Strangely enough, a county mayor named Chau Bian[5] publicly announced that merchants who wanted to do business in his county could set their prices according to the theory of supply and demand. His announcement immediately pleased the merchants, who swarmed into his domain. Soon cartloads of rice flowed in his realm. In a very short period of time, the county was over-supplied. The price of rice dropped to a reasonable levels and many people were saved from starvation.

Build Milestones

Northern Chou Dynasty
557 A.D. to 581 A.D.

With observation and creativity you may find practices that, while not pressing, can be improved. This story happened in the six century A.D. during the Northern Chou dynasty, an unfortuante time of disunity for China. In those days, the roads were marked by milestones, which were made out of earth. These milestones needed to be repaired or even reconstructed every three or four years, according to their condition. A newly-appointed military governor, Woei Shiaw-Kuan,[6] one day noticed that the milestones were easily wrecked and the maintenance and construction costs were high.

Contemplating the problem for a long while, he ordered his subordinates to replace those weatherbeaten milestones with pagoda trees, which were inexpensive to plant and maintain. Travelers could rest themselves under the shade of the trees, and peddlers could set up their stands nearby, to sell snacks and trinkets, which would boost the local economy.

Prime Minister Yuwin Tai[7] heard what this governor was doing and praised him for his ingenuity. "What a clever idea! He identifies a problem, and in solving it he saves money for the central government, encourages local business, and assists travelers. How can we let this creative idea stay in only one province?" A few days later, the prime minister issued an ordinance stating that earthen milestones would be replaced by pagoda trees on all roads in the country.

Plant Mulberry Trees

Northern Sung Dynasty
970 A.D. to 1127 A.D.

How can you influence people to persuade them to do what you want? Generally speaking, there are three ways: you can demand that they do what you want, encourage them to do what you want, or trick them into doing it. A mayor from the Northern Sung dynasty demonstrated the efficiency of the second method.

Newly-appointed mayor Fan Chwen-Zan[8] wanted to promote the silk industry in his domain, but the majority of his constituency were farmers. He could play hard-ball and order the farmers to give up their regular crops and plant mulberry trees, which were necessary for silk production, and penalize those who disobeyed. However, they would grumble and react with great reluctance, which would directly affect both the productivity and the mayor's reputation. He could also trick them into planting the trees. But they might eventually discover the trick and feel deceived. The bond of trust between him and his people would be ruined. His words would no longer be respected. Therefore, as a clever and far-sighted master, he decided to encourage people.

After carefully studying all of the human resources that were under his absolute control, he declared that anyone convicted of a misdemeanor could plant mulberry trees in their backyards instead of performing hard labor, as was the normal punishment. The number of trees to be planted depended on the seriousness of one's violation. Their sentences could also be reduced according to the cultivation of the allotted trees.

What an innovative concept! Who would choose being confined in a jail and treated as an animal? All of the minor offenders preferred this light task to a jail sentence or physical punishment. In a few years, there were thousands of fully-grown mulberry trees available, and local citizens started to breed silkworms, which brought in handsome profits. People admired the mayor and praised him for the wealth that his clever idea brought to the region.

Redirect idle human resources to other useful fields. You will be surprised by the result.

Give Them a Hand
Ming Dynasty
1368 A.D. to 1644 A.D.

This story occurred in the sixteenth century A.D. A new county mayor named Jang Shiu[9] observed many jobless persons idling around the streets. They sometimes disturbed other people and their existence certainly tarnished the image of the county. Furthermore, the government spent money providing food, clothing, and other charitable items. Deciding this was an urgent issue, the mayor carefully studied the problem for many days until he came up with a solution.

With a public decree, the mayor generously supplied the jobless people with public farmland, seeds, pigs, and chickens, and instructed them to cultivate the land. He granted this privilege with obligations. If the recipients didn't take proper care of their possessions, they would be arrested and charged with fraud and idleness. Most were thrilled and deeply appreciated the mayor for this precious opportunity.

For those who declined to accept it, he constantly dispatched policemen to harass them, charge them with idleness, and take them to jail. Those few loafers who didn't want to work and also didn't want to be harassed any more, relocated themselves to other regions. In less than two years, not a single loafer appeared in his domain.

Poverty can deprive a person of dignity and crush a person's ambition. Everyone needs an opportunity to try and prove their usefulness. If given a chance, most people will cherish an opportunity, and with persistence work their way up out of poverty's grasp.

PART THREE

Observant Wisdom

As an old saying goes, "It is an ill omen if, standing on a cliff and looking down into a river, you can see fish in the deep water." Why is this an ill omen? Because by knowing too much, the average person will inevitably conjure troubles and eventually harm him or herself.

On the other hand, this saying does not apply to an enterprising person, who likes to explore dangerous and uncharted territories. Such a person must possess keen senses and a certain quality of persistence. Dangers and threats, for this person, are challenges that represent rare-found opportunities. Without confronting and overcoming challenges, an ambitious person is indistinguishable from the masses, who unrealistically dream about living forever undisturbed.

Being both brave and perceptive, the enterprising person is constantly seeking advancement. Wisdom does not come from birth, but through practice and experience. By continuously sharpening his or her intelligence, an ambitious person will not be dejected or frightened by approaching troubles, as mundane people usually are. As a matter of fact, conflict is welcomed, even sought out. The enterprising person knows that even in failure, some valuable lesson is learned. And in success, competence is proved and wit is polished. Thus, with either result, he or she is a winner by meeting the challenge.

The greatest difference between an average person and a leader is attitude in a crisis. The former will be worried; the later, confident. To illustrate this point, here are some well-known events from Chinese history.

CHAPTER NINE

Sharp and Penetrating

A False Accusation

Tang Dynasty
618 A.D. to 907 A.D.

Have you ever been wrongfully accused? What do you feel? Anger and frustration are most people's reactions. It is a terrible experience. Your reputation is at stake and people begin to doubt your word. How could you clear your name and outsmart the accuser? An interesting episode from the early seventh century A.D.

In the old days, government officials often differed over political philosophy and grouped themselves into factions. To win the trust of their master, they would slyly attempt to discredit others. To create vacancies for themselves, they would work to bring down a high-ranking opponent.

Once, a well-known and very loyal military governor, General Lee Gin,[1] who supervised many border cities, was wrongfully accused of conspiring against the empire. It was a delicate and urgent matter because the general managed most of the country's best soldiers. If this allegation were true, the dynasty would be in great danger. This general, a military genius, could march on the capital city or defect to an enemy camp. Furthermore, even his innocence was proved, the commander's distinguished reputation would be tarnished by the inquiry. As a result, he would be promoted to a prestigious but powerless position or be forced to resign, and the nation would lose the services of a great officer. This accusation, even as yet unproved, could bring disaster.

Emperor Tang-Gau[2] was distressed by this accusation and immediately dispatched a very shrewd commissioner, acting as a censor, to investigate it. The censor, suspecting the conspiracy charge was false, insisted that the accuser accompany him on this truth-finding journey. Without any hesitation, the emperor permitted his request.

To uphold the tranquillity of the dynasty, the censor's identity was disguised and the purpose of the trip became top secret. After a day's travel, the commissioner declared that he had lost all the documents relating to the case. He loudly scolded his assistants for their 'carelessness,' and courteously asked the accuser to re-write the whole complaint against the general, which he did.

Carefully comparing this new statement with the original, which he hadn't lost at all, the censor discovered several contradictions. He presented these discrepancies to the accuser, who was shocked and, after a brief resistance, admitted that he concocted the whole incident. Putting him under arrest, the commissioner returned to the city and reported the outcome of the case.

Without hesitation the emperor ordered the accuser to be executed, and the whole event was carefully concealed until years later, when the information was safe to release.

A truth can always be told again and again with accuracy, but a lie holds contradictions. A careful and clever probe will reveal them.

Other's is Better
Northern Sung Dynasty
960 A.D. to 1279 A.D.

As an old Chinese saying goes, "Standing on a hilltop, you always look up and believe the next hill is higher, although they are equal in altitude." This saying represents a typical human belief that something you don't have is always better than something you do have. If you were a judge, how would you deal with this belief? This amusing episode occurred during the Northern Sung dynasty.

A very famous and affluent official died and left equal portions of his wealth to his two daughters and their sons-in-law. However, there were no precise prices on the land and homes that he passed on to them, each of which had a unique market value. Dissatisfied with the arrangement, each daughter believed the other party got the lion's share.

After the grandiose burial ceremony, the daughters filed civil lawsuits against each other, claiming that their own shares were less than the other's. In court, the judge Jang Chi-Shan[3] asked them, one after the other, whether they thought that they were treated unfairly. They each gave a firm "Yes." The clerk recorded every word and let sign all the statements. The judge then asked them to provide an inventory and turn in a list all of the inherited properties. They gladly complied with this request. After they finished, he announced his decree; "These two daughters must exchange their inheritances with one another." The daughters were shocked. Each had hoped to gain more than the other. However, they could do nothing but accept this ruling.

What an interesting lawsuit and a smart decree. The judge outwitted them with their own greed.

Whose Son?

Western Han Dynasty
206 B.C. to 25A.D.

Once there were two women who argued over a son. Both claimed to be his natural mother. In the old days, because a woman's social status was so low, she had to depend on a husband or a son to support her, so the question of motherhood was important. To complicate the matter, both parties had many loyal witnesses. If you were a judge, what would you do?

This incident happened in the Western Han dynasty. Two brothers lived together. Both their wives were pregnant and gave birth at about the same time. The elder brother's son died during delivery, so he stole his younger brother's newborn child. The younger brother was infuriated and promptly filed a civil lawsuit.

Both parties had witnesses, who swore on their honesty in front of the gods, to support each claim. This case dragged on for three years. Many mayors examined the case and couldn't reach a decision. This news of this spread all over the country, and eventually reached the capital city and the ears of Prime Minister Hwan Ba,[4] who was famous for his shrewdness. The prime minister demanded that this intricate litigation be transferred to his jurisdiction.

In a few days, the plaintiffs and the defendants were summoned to a court in the capital. Curious citizens swarmed there from all over the country to see if this clever judge could unravel such a tangled case. In front of several thousand bystanders, the prime minister instructed a large and muscular bodyguard to hold the disputed child tightly in his arms. He then told the two wives to stand ten paces away from this guard, one on each side. Finally, he ordered the women to grab the child, and declared that whoever successfully pulled him from the bodyguard's muscular grasp could keep the child.

With obvious excitement, the elder brother's wife dashed forward and mercilessly took hold of the child, intending to use all her strength to jerk the baby free. The real mother, who was afraid to hurt her baby, touched him gently and then, with a look of great mourning, immediately released him. "Stop this farce!" the prime minister shouted at the top of voice. Seeing how the woman was unwilling to risk harming the child, he rightly concluded that she must be the real mother.

To detect a falsehood, you must have a deep understanding of human nature, and must shrewdly scrutinize both words and actions.

Divide It In Two

Ming Dynasty,
1368 A.D. to 1644 A.D.

One day, a mayor named Fan Tai[5] saw two men heatedly quarreling over a bolt of cotton cloth. Curious, he approached the men and questioned them. Each one claimed sole ownership of the merchandise. After hearing their complaints, the mayor ordered his bodyguards to cut the cloth into two equal portions. The men were surprised by this quick action. With indignation, they stared at one another, and then reluctantly departed, each holding half bolt of the cloth. Then, the mayor directed his aides to quietly tail the men and observe their behavior. Later, the aides reported that one of them was full of delight and the other was very gloomy. The mayor immediately ordered his guards to arrest the cheerful one. After brief trial, the arrested man admitted that the cloth was not rightfully his.

When good fortune unexpectedly drops into a person's lap, he will be very happy. On the other hand, a stroke of bad luck will dishearten a person, and his face will be filled with sadness and anxiety. The honest person, who forfeited half of his cloth, felt miserable. On the contrary, the crook, who gained without toil, was exuberant. With some common sense and keen observation, the mayor cleverly resolved this quarrel.

The Obvious Murderer

Ming Dynasty
1368 A.D. to 1644 A.D.

Be cautious and observant. As an old saying goes, "You will never tumble over a huge mountain but a tiny bump." Another way to put it is that you are always aware of your enemies, but rarely do you keep an eye on intimate friends. Yet an intimate friend would most easily be able to hurt you. A homicide case from the Ming dynasty demonstrates this idea.

A man named Ju Kai[6] was killed in a well-known temple more than twenty miles away from his home. The murder was committed in the pitch-dark night and there was no witness. Furthermore, that location was away from the victim's usual routes. After a few days of fruitless investigation, the mayor, Yin Yuen-Gi,[7] one day received an anonymous letter accusing one of the victim's colleagues of the crime.

The accused man was known to be hot-tempered and had many opponents, so almost all of the mayor's aides believed the accusation, despite the lack of direct evidence.

"Good fortune will not easily drop into my lap. I don't believe this letter." the mayor coldly remarked. He questioned the victim's family members about the victim's daily activities and the names of his intimate friends. They said that a clerk, working in city hall, was his best friend. Returning to his office, the mayor ordered his aides to assemble all the clerks. He claimed that he wanted to select two clerks among them to copy some documents for him, and courteously requested them to duplicate a full page of text. After they finished, he collected and meticulously studied those samples, carefully comparing them with the anonymous letter. He found that the intimate friend's handwriting precisely matched the unsigned letter.

The mayor dispatched a squad of policemen to arrest the clerk. After a few hours of searching, the clerk was located and brought under guard to the court. The mayor showed him the evidence. Shocked, with sweat rapidly rolling down from his forehead, the clerk knelt and confessed.

"I knew the victim for years. A few days ago, he wanted to travel out of town to purchase some merchandise. As his best friend, I accompanied him to the temple. He showed me his money. Having an urgent debt to pay off, I humbly asked him to lend me some, which he flatly refused. He even mocked me for asking. Out of anger and greed, I attacked him and killed him on the spot."

Be aware of your companions. Of course you would be cautious with a total stranger, but a life-long friend may catch you off-guard and take advantage of your trust.

Cut Him Down to Size

Eastern Han Dynasty
25 A.D. to 220 A.D.

As an old saying goes, "Even a powerful dragon can't subdue a snake hiding in the earth." It means that no matter how influential and powerful you are, you have to pay some respect to those beneath you. In the old days, a newly-appointed official would often be mocked by experienced subordinates, who had been in their positions for years. To demonstrate who really was in charge, they would routinely attempt to embarrass their new superior and cut him down to size. On the other hand, if the newcomer outmaneuvered these attempts, he would instantly earn the respect of his subordinates.

Overhearing that the newly-appointed mayor Zou Yu[8] was strict with his juniors, a crafty deputy mayor wanted to embarrass him. He stole a corpse from an obscure graveyard on the outskirts of the city, cut off its limbs and placed it in front of the mayor's office. Arriving in his domain, the new mayor was cordially welcomed by all of his subordinates. They courteously ushered him to the city hall.

Everyone was surprised to see a grotesque torso on the door. The mayor immediately discerned the trick as an attempt to humiliate him on his first day. Holding back his temper, he calmly approached the corpse and pretended to initiate a friendly conversation with it in an inaudible fashion.

The attendants were amazed. Some stood there dumbly, and dared not interfere or utter a word of comment. Other officials forcefully restrained their laughter and shook their heads, clandestinely praising the deputy mayor for his creative trick. How could the mayor possibly resolve this case? They reckoned that his reputation would be completely ruined.

Beaming a confident smile and chatting casually, the mayor scrutinized the corpse and noticed some dried grass on the skin. Seeing that, he turned his head and looked sternly at his juniors. He loudly promised to the body that he would find out the person who 'invited' him.

After everyone departed, the mayor carefully studied a local map and, with an old native servant's assistance, located several neglected graveyards. Then, the shrewd mayor privately summoned all the guards who were responsible for policing the gates near those sites, and asked them if they had seen anybody transporting dried grass into the city recently. One gate-keeper recalled that the deputy mayor had a cartload delivered two days ago. The mayor immediately dispatched his bodyguards to arrest that official. They thoroughly searched his residence and found some evidence against him. After hours of grilling, the ill-humored deputy mayor finally confessed his misconduct and, after a public trial, was penalized according to the law. That news rapidly spread all over the city. Local citizens were astounded by the new mayor's shrewdness. After that incident, none of his subordinates dared to challenge his authority.

Keep calm when faced with a surprise. Your disquiet is expected and will only satisfy your opponents and expose your vulnerability.

Recreate the Scene

Three Kingdoms Period 220 A.D. to 280 A.D.

In the old days, people depended on fire for heat and light. They used open fires to cook their foods and warm their homes, and used candles and soybean lamps to brighten dark nights. However, great calamities were also caused by fire, because ordinary people lived in houses made from hay and earth, which made them extremely susceptible to fire. But sometimes, a devastating blaze was not caused by accident.

Once there was a wife who poisoned her husband. To cover up her crime, she set fire to her kitchen. Neighbors saw the flames and tried to extinguish it. However, because of a water shortage, the whole house rapidly burned to the ground. Clearing the site, they found her husband's blackened corpse. Seeing the dead body, the wife wept and sobbed, claiming that her husband had burned to death. In that era, it was a reasonable explanation for such a misfortune. However, her husband's young brother was suspicious. He accused the wife of murder and filed a complaint with the local authority.

Carefully reviewing this case, Mayor Jang Jeu,[9] acting as a judge, gathered all the relatives in the court and ordered his assistants to bring in two young pigs. The hall was packed with curious onlookers. They wondered why the mayor was wasting time on such a clear-cut case. The mayor directed his assistants to tie up the two animals, place them on two separate haystacks in the front yard of the city hall, and slaughter one of the pigs.

People were puzzled. Was he trying to barbecue those two miserable animals with hay? What kind of dish would that be? Curious local citizens swarmed to the courtyard and jammed the streets. Some even climbed onto nearby roofs to get a better look at this strange show.

After a brief announcement about the lawsuit, the mayor commanded his guards to set fire to the two haystacks. The living pig's piercing and hopeless screams filled the air. The crowd watched in noiseless fascination.

When the fires burned themselves out, the mayor directed his assistants to examine the pigs' mouths. The mouth of pig who was burned alive was stuffed with half-burned hay and ash, but the slaughtered pig's tongue and teeth were spotless. This condition matched the husband's mouth, which was free of hay and ash. From this test, it was easy to conclude that the husband was dead before the fire. His wife was arrested, and after hours of questioning confessed her crime.

Slip of Words

Ming Dynasty
1368 A.D. to 1644 A.D.

In the old days, virtuous women were not supposed to step out of their houses. Shopping in a market was a female servant's job. As a custom, when visiting a neighbor and knocking on their door, you always called out the husband's name. This custom became an important clue during a murder case that took place long ago in Southern China.

Mr. Chao,[5] a merchant, planned a business trip down the river with one of his friends. However, his wife insisted that he must cancel this engagement and stay home. They quarreled for days. On the morning of the business trip, after another verbal skirmish, the merchant angrily left home and arrived hours early at the small boat he was to travel on. Holding a hundred ounces of silver coins in a handbag, he felt sleepy and took a nap in the cabin.

Seeing all that silver, Jang Chau,[10] the boatman, who knew Mr. Chao, slowly sailed the vessel to an obscure location. Cautiously looking around to ensure that no other boats were in the area, he entered the room and, after fetching a weapon, slaughtered the rich merchant with a broad-blade knife and dumped his body into the river among tall bushy reeds. Then, he hid the money in a safe place and casually navigated the boat back to its regular spot, where he pretended to fall into a deep sleep.

A few moments later, the merchant's partner arrived. Not seeing his friend, he went to wait in the cabin. After an hour, he was deeply annoyed. He gently shook the boatman awake and asked him to look for his friend. Without hesitation, the boatman ran to the merchant's home. Knocking at his door, he shouted, "Madam Chao!" and then loudly asked about her husband. With amazement, she answered that he had left home hours ago. He returned and told Mr. Chao's partner, who was astonished. He hurriedly went to visit and confirm that news. After brief discussion with Madam Chao, the pair decided to search for him. For three fatiguing days they anxiously scoured the city but couldn't find him, so they called on the local authority and reported it.

Reviewing this report, the mayor suspected the merchant's wife. He immediately dispatched servants to stalk her. After weeks of investigation and surveillance, they found no evidence of her guilt. He then thought that the man was killed by a highwayman, and ordered the regional police force to search for and arrest a suspect, but none could be found.

One day, a new assistant read the case and confidently remarked that the boatman was the true murderer. Astounded, his superior asked him about the reason.

"It is obvious." he explained. "The boatman already knew the merchant wasn't home. Otherwise, he wouldn't shout 'Madam Chao.'" Accepting this theory, the mayor complimented the assistant for his keen observation. He abruptly issued a warrant to arrest that boatman for questioning. The boatman was brought to the court and thoroughly interrogated by the mayor. After hours of dodging questions and giving evasive answers, the boatman came to the end of his wits and confessed his crime.

Be all ears. One can learn the truth from a slip of words.

Hidden Gold Nuggets

Tang Dynasty
618 A.D. to 907 A.D.

A farmer working in his rice field one day dug up an urn full of gold nuggets. With excitement, he reported this find to the local authority, and after an official came out to inspect the gold, the farmer requested that they safeguard it for him. Hearing this request, the mayor, out of benevolence, said he would be responsible for keeping the urn and the nuggets safe. So the farmer delivered the urn to the mayor's mansion.

Two days later, the mayor checked on the urn and was surprised to find that it was filled with bricks. How could solid gold simply disappear? The official labels were still on the urn, and there was no sign of a break-in. Greatly embarrassed, this ill-fated official, who couldn't provide a rational explanation, was charged with embezzlement and held at the local jail. Investigators were unable to collect enough evidence to either convict him or prove his innocence, so he had to remain in jail.

Word of this mystery rapidly spread. Local citizens zealously discussed the case and formulated their own theories. As the investigation dragged on, no new evidence was uncovered. The county mayor in charge of the case was depressed about his inability to find a solution. It was becoming an embarrassment. The credibility of all regional officials was at stake. He wished someone would voluntarily assume this strange lawsuit, but no one dared to jeopardize their reputation.

At a private party some months later, the governor of the region sadly mentioned this bizarre case. Yuan Ze,[12] one of the governor's aides lowered his head and contemplated for a moment. Then he said "I believe the mayor is innocent and I would like to take this case." His request was instantly granted. The county mayor gladly transferred this troublesome litigation to him.

After carefully reviewing the report, Yuan Ze visited a goldsmith, borrowed the same amount of gold nuggets that the farmer had reported, and loaded them in an identical urn. Summoning the farmer, who was accompanied by many curious citizens, Yuan Ze ordered two muscular men to carry the urn down the road. They failed the task miserably, unable to even move it an inch. The urn was too heavy for a pair of men to lift. However, according to the court transcript, two farmers carried it to the mayor's home. All the bystanders then understood that the urn was switched before arriving at its final destination. The governor's aide immediately issued a warrant to arrest those two farmers, and the mayor was released on the spot.

Examine a case carefully. You must scrutinize every detail. In any fraud there are always inconsistencies and contradictions. With common sense and some deduction, you can root them out and prove the truth.

Whose Jacket?
Northern Wei Dynasty
386 A.D. to 534 A.D.

Attention to detail helped solve this case from the Northern Wei dynasty.

A woodcutter and a salt-peddler once took a rest under the shade of the same pagoda tree. Upon departure, they quarreled over a sheepskin jacket. Each one claimed that the jacket belonged to him. Curious bystanders gathered round, to try and help sort out the problem, but no one could settle the dispute. As a result, they sought out the local authority.

After briefly listening to both sides, the mayor Lee Huai,[13] who was obviously bored by the simplicity of the litigation, casually remarked, "What an unchallenging case. It is very simple to determine."

He then ordered his guards to beat the jacket with rods. Some bits of salt fell from the sheepskin. All the onlookers were deeply impressed by the official's shrewdness. The astonished woodcutter lowered his head and admitted the crime.

In those days, people were so woven into a trade that it would be reflected even in their clothes. The clever mayor kept this fact in mind, and used it to find a simple solution.

CHAPTER TEN

Expose the Vicious

Fistfight

Northern Sung Dynasty
960 A.D. to 1127 A.D.

In a homicide case, people often suspect the victim's enemy and overlook the people closest to him. This sometimes leads to a wrong conclusion, as the following story demonstrates.

In a bar, two drunkards were quarreling. The argument degenerated into a violent fist fight. After a few furious blows the combatants were separated by a group of bystanders. After the fight, each one of them stumbled home and fell to sleep.

At midnight, the crescent moon spread its murky light dimly over the surface of the earth. A shadow approached the house of one of the drunkards and slipped into the bedroom. The sharp blade of an ax flashed in the moonlight, and the drunkard screamed. Both of his feet had been chopped off! The drunkard screamed again, cursing and accusing the man who had fought with him that evening. The drunkard's wife woke their neighbors. Some went to fetch a doctor while others tried to stop the bleeding, but it was hopeless. The victim quickly died of blood loss. His wife went to the local authority and tearfully reported the horrible murder.

Some marshals captured the other drunkard and brought him to jail, where he was personally interrogated by mayor Yuen Gian.[1] The mayor then went to examine the body and console the victim's wife.

"Madam," he appeased, "don't worry. The suspect already admitted his crime. He will pay for it dearly. Your husband's case is closed."

He went back to the jail and clandestinely sent a team of spies to watch her and her house around the clock. They recorded every person who made contact with her. Several days later, the wife and a monk were arrested. After hours of interrogation, they finally confessed their adultery and this homicide. The drunkard, who had been passed out in bed at the time of the murder, was released. The two adulterers were charged with first degree murder, and after a short court session, sentenced to death.

During a private occasion, one of the mayor's aides asked about the case. "Why did you suspect the victim's wife, his trusted partner?"

"It is plain and simple," the mayor remarked with a profound smile. "An argument and fist fight is hardly enough of a motive for murder. However, someone might use this incident to shield their own wicked behavior. Furthermore, I detected that the wife's lamenting was insincere. From her unemotional weeping and sobbing, I sensed that she was rather pleased about this tragedy. And there was another clue. While the victim was covered in blood, his wife, who was sharing the bed, didn't get one bloodstain on her clothes. From those details, I was sure that the man had been murdered by his wife's lover."

What a shrewd and observant official! He truly understood one of the human's basic rules: The most trustworthy person is the only one capable of totally breaking your heart because that person has already won your confidence.

Create Conflicts

Western Han Dynasty
206 B.C. to 25 A.D.

How can one person compete successfully against a group? The worst strategy is to confront all of them head-on. The best method is to create conflicts among them. Let them distrust and attack one another so that they waste their energy and resources. A clever official successfully used this strategy to halt lawlessness in his district.

In those days, noblemen rarely respected the law. Holding both political and financial power, they became arrogant and ruthless, and openly committed many crimes and violations. No government officials wanted to be assigned to the districts where the lawless noblemen lived. However, a county mayor named Chau Kwan-Han[2] thought otherwise. He confidently received his new appointment and arrived on the outskirts of the capital city, where many of those lawless aristocrats lived.

For the first several months, the new mayor privately dispatched many servants to record those noblemen's violations. He also spent lots of time studying and understanding the wealthy families and their relationships with the central government and local politicians. After thoroughly comprehending the situation, he began to issue warrants against less-influential family members. Furthermore, during the trials, he deliberately revealed that those arrests were solely due to the assistance of the defendants' opponents. This information immediately created friction between families. No matter how the trail turned out, the defendants would abhor their rivals for the rest of their lives. As a result, they instructed their servants to snoop around and expose the wrongdoings of their rivals so they would have to visit the court and justify themselves. Dumping money into lawsuits and briberies, the families eventually exhausted themselves financially, and some were completely wrecked.

To agitate the situation even further, the mayor ordered a carpenter to construct a wooden complaint box, which he placed in the front yard of the city hall. He encouraged local citizens to expose any corrupt or illegal conduct. Upon receiving the letters, he would react promptly, sending policemen to arrest and detain the accused. During the interrogation, he would intentionally indicate that the complaint had come from the persons' foes, which was not true at all. However, those accused noblemen sought to get even with their opponents. In less than a year, most of the wealthy and unscrupulous noblemen in his domain were vigorously fighting one another. Their wicked influence was greatly reduced. To give their opponents no basis for complaint, they dared not to infringe upon the law any more. The tranquillity of the society was properly restored.

As an old saying goes, "Two fists can hardly compete with four hands." To successfully subdue many strong opponents, you must rely on your intelligence. Create friction among your enemies. Let them kill themselves off. As a result, you can easily defeat those who remain and claim the final victory.

A Shrewd Inspector   *Ming Dynasty*
                                        1368 A.D. to 1644 A.D.

There was once a well-known police inspector named Jang Shau-Sher.[4] He was famous for his extremely keen observation. Once, on a sizzling-hot summer afternoon, the inspector was casually strolling through a famous temple. By chance, he saw three men sleeping in a corner of the left wing of the temple. Next to the men was a watermelon that had been sliced into several pieces but not eaten.

The inspector directed his aides to arrest the men for burglary and bring them back to the station. After brief interrogation, they confessed their wrongdoing.

"How could that be?" asked the amazed local citizens when they heard of this incident. "It is incredible! The inspector is more than gifted. His instinct is too sharp to believe."

During a private party, one of his colleagues inquired about this amazing display of deduction. Beaming a profound smile the inspector explained "It is nothing. I am merely detail-oriented and mindful. With some common sense you also could discover lots of significant things happening around you."

"Generally speaking, law-abiding persons start work at dawn and go to bed at dusk. Seeing three able-bodied men dozing at noon immediately raised my suspicion. Furthermore, most people cut open a watermelon and immediately enjoy it. These men didn't do so. Instead, they deliberately opened that juicy melon to attract flies, which would keep those nasty insects from disturbing their slumber. That kind of luxurious arrangement might take place in the bedroom of a wealthy mansion, but not in a public place. Their plain clothes indicated that they didn't belong to any privileged social class, so how could they afford to be so wasteful? They must have acquired lots of extra money."

"With this in mind I reasoned that they must have recently committed some crimes. After vigorously questioning them and searching their houses, I successfully confirmed my suspicion." His piercing analysis was highly praised by everyone at the party.

Close Relationship

Northern Sung Dynasty
960 A.D. to 1127 A.D.

In most homicide cases, the relationship between the victim and the murderer is often close. In the old days, people were grouped geographically. They usually lived in the same village for generations, and knew one another intimately. Any cautious investigator, regardless of the obvious suspect, must collect the victim's background information and carefully analyze it. Otherwise, he might miss the real murderer.

Once a traveling monk wanted to stay in a rich man's house. He courteously knocked at the door and expressed his intention. Due to the visitor's shabby dress, the host disdainfully refused to accept him. The monk politely persisted, so the wealthy host reluctantly allowed him to stay in the stable. The traveler kindly thanked him and went to make a bed out of hay. The tired monk fell rapidly into deep sleep.

At midnight, he was awakened by a sudden noise. Peering out of the stable, he saw two figures, one male and one female, hurriedly climbing down the wall. From the girl's clothing, he was certain that she was a maid in the service of the wealthy family. Obviously, she was running away with her lover. Frightened, the monk reckoned that if the unsympathetic host found out that a female servant was gone, he would quite possibly be blamed. Anxiously contemplating the possible outcomes, he decided to take his leave. Walking quickly through the darkness, he fell straight into an old well. Even more to his amazement, he landed right on the maid's dead body. She had been murdered! The luckless monk had badly hurt his ankle in the fall, and couldn't move an inch. He began to moan.

In the morning, servants overheard the woeful sound and followed to its source. They discovered him and the dead maid. Pulling him out, the servants delivered the monk to the local authority. Besides accusing him of murder, the host also submitted an inventory of missing jewelry. What a simple case! They had a suspect, the victim's body and, after severe physical torture, a written confession. The mayor, after a speedy trial, sentenced the monk to death regardless of the fact that both the murder weapon and stolen jewels couldn't be found.

Upon reviewing this case, the county mayor Shan Min-Zon doubted the monk's confession. It was inconsistent and even contradictory in several places. He summoned one of his ablest marshals, gave him meticulous instructions for a ruse to seek out more evidence, and then clandestinely dispatched him to investigate the case.

The marshal arrived in the village and checked into the local tavern. Observing his appearance, the experienced hostess correctly guessed his identity, and cordially made conversation with him. After brief amenities, she learned that homicide case was concluded. The marshal said he had come here to deliver the written confirmation. The monk would be executed in days.

"Even if the real killer is caught at this very moment," the marshal, who seemed to be heavily intoxicated, loudly proclaimed, "he won't be charged with any misconduct at all. Those officials are all shameless and self-centered pigs. They know they have the wrong man, but they want to end this investigation quickly. They'd never admit they made a mistake."

Beaming a mysterious smile, the hostess murmured to herself "What a clever devil!" Hearing this, the marshal dropped his drunken act and arrested the woman. After a severe interrogation, she revealed that the girl had actually been murdered by a young villager. He had tricked her into falling in love with him, then convinced her to steal some valuables and run away with him. However, his real intention was to possess the jewelry, not her. Once she came to him with the jewels, he stabbed her to death.

Learning the whole story, the law enforcer immediately went to the local authority, disclosed his identity and the hostess's confession, and directed them to catch that suspect. The local police dutifully followed his orders. They promptly located, surrounded, and raided the suspect's house. The real murderer was captured by total surprise and his house thoroughly searched. They found the murdering knife and all the stolen goods. The evidence was conclusive. He was charged with murder, after a fair trial, and received the death sentence. The innocent monk was released.

No Recognition

Ming Dynasty
1368 A.D. to 1644 A.D.

In ancient times, well-behaved girls, especially from wealthy families, rarely stepped out their front doors. Their social activity was confined to their own houses. They were not even allowed to wear clothing that would expose their arms. A crafty thief tried to use this social standard to free himself from capture during the Ming dynasty.

By chance, a burglar sneaked in the bedroom of a newly married couple and hid beneath their well-decorated bed. For three days, he could not find a single opportunity to steal any valuable items, or even to escape. Finally, starved to the edge of death, he feebly crawled out from his hiding place and was abruptly detected and captured by male servants. The father of the family ordered them to send the intruder to the local authority.

Arriving at the court, the burglar falsely claimed that he was the girl's family doctor, and that she had an odd disease and needed him to take care of her now and then. With skepticism, the judge asked him about the bride's family background. Having been in the house for three days, the thief had picked up enough information to correctly answer all the judge's questions. Unable to prove that this man was not the girl's doctor, the official decided to let the bride confront him in court.

That decision might seem reasonable now. However, at that time, society was very conservative. Simply having to appear in court, for whatever reason, would ruin her and her family's reputation. Knowing this, the crafty burglar reckoned that the wealthy plaintiffs, to uphold their reputation, would drop their complaint and let him go.

That night, the victim's father anxiously visited an aged clerk, who had worked in the court for over twenty years. He was very experienced in complicated cases.

After carefully listening to the dilemma, the clerk calmly remarked "What a shameless crook! He knows that you will not allow your daughter to face the public at any cost. Betting on that, he thinks he'll soon be released. But I've got a clever trick, if you're willing." He whispered a trick into the wealthy visitor's ear. Hearing that, the father smiled with satisfaction, thanked the clerk and departed.

On the court day, he hired a prostitute, dressed her up to the prosperous family's standard, and gave her some instructions. The thief was waiting in the courtroom. When he saw the well-dressed woman enter, he loudly declared, "That is she. I have treated your illness for years. Why did your family accuse me of being an outlaw?"

However, unknown to the thief, the bride's father had revealed the scheme to the judge, who observed the thief's reaction and beamed a profound smile, inwardly admiring the clerk for his cleverness. The judge disclosed the trick out loud and in detail. Hearing this, all the observers spontaneously burst into roars of hilarious laughter. The burglar was dumbfounded. He knew he had no choice but to admit his crime.

What a smart trick! The burglar's falsehood was revealed by his own declaration.

The Magic Barley Seeds

*Southern Sung Dynasty
1127 A.D. to 1279 A.D.*

Mayor Hu Gi-Zon[5] was once traveling through his domain. His coach was stopped by an old woman, who was visiting a nearby and well-known temple. She bitterly complained that her overcoat had been stolen. Patiently listening to her tedious and monotonous protest, the official ordered his aides to alter his schedule and head for the temple. In a few moments, they arrived.

After gathering a group of old women around him and revealing his purpose, the mayor took out a small bag of barley seeds.

"Ladies," he addressed them, "I know and believe all of you are honorable, pious persons. Please hold some of those magic seeds in your palms, close your eyes and repeat some incantations after me. The real thief's seeds will be cultivated and grow sprouts." He then dispatched all of his guards to give a handful of seeds to the old women.

With religious sincerity, they faithfully followed his directions. He quoted some lines from a sacred volume. Almost all of the women tightly shut their eyes and tranquilly repeated the prayers sentence by sentence. However, one old woman standing in a far corner, looked riddled with anxiety. She narrowed her eyes and frequently peeked through her palms, nervously checking the seeds.

Observing this, the mayor made a gesture towards the old woman. His bodyguards promptly seized her. After a speedy search, they uncovered the stolen item. She shamefully lowered her head and admitted her wrongdoing.

Judge It at Midnight

Ming Dynasty
1368 A.D. to 1644 A.D.

A mid-level official was informed that his concubine had been murdered. Shocked, he went home and confirmed the tragedy. This homicide was reported to the local authority. They immediately dispatched policemen to arrest that official, who was more confused than frightened. A censor named Young Fen-Chuen[6] was assigned to handle this case. He intentionally detained the suspect in the jail for over two weeks, allowed him no visitors, and instructed his aides not to release any information. Then, fabricating a plausible excuse, this shrewd judge announced that the court session would be at midnight, and all observers were prohibited. At the designated date, he casually questioned the official, who calmly answered all the questions.

Prior to the trial, this censor clandestinely directed some of his bodyguards to dress as local citizens and to hide outside. They were to round up anyone who came snooping around the courthouse during the midnight session. They detained less than a dozen people. After meticulous questioning, the judge filtered out two suspects, who were kept in jail for the night.

Issuing warrants, he then sent his men to thoroughly search their houses. They returned and reported that one of them possessed some suspicious jewelry, which was identified as belonging to the victim. The man was severely grilled and eventually confessed his wrongdoing.

"How did you know that the real offender would be sneaking around the courthouse?" asked an aide during a private occasion.

"It is very simple," this calculating censor remarked. "The true murderer agonized for over half month while I detained the original suspect and gave out no information about the case. My decree would directly affect his whole life. The uncertainty must have tormented him both day and night. How could he not worry about it? With that in mind, I reasoned that innocent citizens would not be interested in staying up so late just to watch a trial, except the true offender. And I was right."

Use Substitution

Ming Dynasty
1368 A.D. to 1644 A.D.

Any criminals, especially murderers, would pay special attention to the actions of the local authority. At the slightest risk of being exposed, they would become alarmed and relocate to another city. However, they often would return to their native land when they were certain that their safety was secured. How could you create this illusion and lure them to face justice? One clever judge used the following trick:

One dark evening, a girl was anxiously waiting for her lover. Overhearing a noise, she cheerfully opened the door and was attacked and slaughtered by a burglar, who hadn't intended to assault her at all. Frightened by this unexpected atrocity, the killer dropped his knife and fled.

A few moments later, the lover came. Because of the darkness, he didn't see his lover's body, and he tumbled over the victim. He fell and smeared his clothes with blood. Shocked and frightened he abruptly ran away.

The next morning, neighbors discovered this tragedy and reported it to the local authority. In a few days this lover was captured and interrogated. He admitted that he had an affair with the girl but denied committing the murder. Reviewing the report, the judge Liu Zon-Gwai[7] examined the murder weapon, a butcher's knife, and believed his statement.

Coincidentally, there was to be a pig-slaughtering contest in a few days. All of the butchers, from this city and neighboring villages and towns, would attend. The official deliberately fabricated an excuse and ordered the butchers to leave their knifes in the city hall for the night. The butchers complied. That night, the judge took out one of the knives and replaced it with the murder weapon. The next day, all the butchers came to fetch their knifes. A contestant, with obvious indignation, refused to pick up that murder weapon and claimed that that knife was not his. From the marks on the handle, he recognized that it actually belonged to one of his compatriots. They asked this man a few more questions, and soon the judge knew who the true offender was.

He dispatched some marshals, in plainclothes, to call on that butcher. They surprisingly discovered that the suspect had already moved himself elsewhere. They returned and reported it to their superior. Considering this problem for a while, this shrewd mayor decided to play it along with the situation.

A few days later, he made a phony trial and sentenced the innocent lover to capital punishment. His substitute, a robber, was publicly executed several months later. Everybody thought this homicide case was concluded. Overhearing this news, the real offender believed that he had committed a perfect crime and, with inflated confidence, clandestinely snuck back to his native town. He was immediately detected, arrested, and escorted to jail. After a speedy trial he received a death sentence.

The lover, due to his immoral behavior with the victim, was spanked in the court. With bruises and minor flesh wounds, he was released on the spot.

A criminal is often very nervous and suspicious because his life is at stake. Eliminating his suspicion, you can successfully lure him from his hideout and bring him to justice.

Check With the Undertakers

Ming Dynasty
1368 A.D. to 1644 A.D.

Once there was a man who, returning from an out-of-city business trip, discovered that his wife had been murdered in their bedroom. More gruesome still, her head was missing!

Shocked and disgusted, he immediately reported this misfortune to the local authority. Neighbors overheard and rapidly spread news of this horrible tale. In less than a day, the victim's family members heard about the murder and, thinking the husband killed her, came to complain to city hall.

The ill-fated husband was arrested and interrogated. After a severe grilling and much torture, he couldn't bear the pain anymore and was forced to make a false confession.

An aide reviewing the case was skeptical. "We didn't locate the victim's head yet. We must not conclude this case at this stage. Although the wife's family has accused him, I do not believe he is the real murderer. I would like to investigate further."

With reluctance, the mayor permitted him to investigate this case. With his superior's permission, this aide, making up a far-fetched reason, privately threw a party and invited all of the local undertakers to attend. In the middle of this gathering, after a good meal and fine wine had been served, he casually asked if anyone had recently handled any strange assignments.

One man spoke up and said that a week ago he assisted a certain rich man in burying a young servant's body. According to the rich man, the servant had died of a sudden and unknown disease. Strangely enough, the coffin was so light that the undertaker thought it was empty.

Based on this story, the aide got a warrant and directed many policemen to dig up the coffin and examine it. Inside was the head of a woman. They fetched the alleged murderer to identify it. Without hesitation, he observed it and immediately claimed that it was not his wife's head. Hearing his testimony, the mayor abruptly sent his men to search the rich man's mansion, where they discovered the suspect's wife, alive and well. She had been committing adultery with the wealthy man. To cover up their wrongdoing and help the wife leave her husband, the rich man heartlessly murdered one of his female servants and used her body to frame the hapless husband. The clever aide had found the true murderer.

Outwit a Crook

*Five Dynasties Period
907 A.D. to 960 A.D.*

The relationship between a hunter and his prey is very delicate. If you approach a bird with a net, she will be alarmed and immediately fly away. On the other hand, if you charm her with seed, she may happily walk into a trap.

The same theory could be applied to a swindler and his mark. If you found that you had been cheated, how could you get even with the crook? Ordinary people would make a complaint to the local authority. But because it is not a murder or some other dangerous crime, the matter would be treated as a low priority. On the other hand, you might try to swindle him back, like in this amusing episode.

A pawn shop owner named Mulon Yan-Chau,[8] once, while inspecting his inventory, surprisingly detected some phony antiques in his warehouse. They had been pawned as genuine. He cursed the careless clerk who had been fooled. The debtor would never come to pay off the obligation and take those worthless pieces back!

Mulon pondered his options. He could write off the phony antiques as a business loss and report the fraud to the local authority, and then passively wait for them to arrest the criminal. Or, instead of naively hoping that the tide of events would turn in his favor, he could treat it as a challenge and find a plot to outsmart the crook! Contemplating for a long while, he eventually cooked up a scheme.

He clandestinely hired a group of laborers to secretly relocate some of his merchandise to another warehouse during the night. The next morning, he 'discovered' that his store was burglarized and announced that whoever held a receipt could ask for compensation if his belongings were stolen. Then he posted an inventory of the missing items, with the faked antiques near the top of the list. "What a delightful news!" thought the swindler, reading the announcement. "Now I can double my profit." Pretending to be irate over the loss of his valuable property, he brusquely presented his receipt and demanded to be properly compensated.

Confirming the claim, the calculating owner suddenly showed a face of chill contempt and sternly ordered his servants to detain the swindler, who was promptly escorted to a police station and charged with fraud.

What a clever scheme! As an old saying goes, "Birds will forfeit their lives due to gluttony, and people due to greed." Thoroughly understanding the mind of a con man, the owner beat the swindler at his own game.

PART FOUR

Dauntless Intelligence

Successful decisions require intelligence and braveness. Intelligence will provide you with a clearly-defined objective and show you the way to achieve it. Braveness will help you take action and execute your plans. Intelligence is like an emperor who gives orders, and braveness is like the assistants who carry out those orders. A person utilizes both qualities in different proportions, and each quality can be developed.

But which is most important? Intelligence. A smart person can learn to develop bravery, but bravery cannot create wisdom. Bravery, like fire, can be useful, but if not governed wisely it can also be destructive. So how do you improve your intelligence? It will not happen by chance. You have to learn, by studying others' experiences and gaining your own. Then you will naturally cultivate penetrating observations and sophisticated thinking. Here are some stories, in two categories, which demonstrate my philosophy.

CHAPTER ELEVEN

Brave and Bold

To Top Your Peers

Eastern Han Dynasty
25 A.D. to 220 A.D.

Do you want to be a hero? How can you outshine your peers? This interesting episode may provide some answers. It happened in the first century A.D.

A government clerk Mr. Ban Chau,[1] whose duty was to duplicate official documents, a tedious and mundane chore, one day threw the bamboo brush away and sighed, "What a lousy job! I've had enough. I don't want to be a clerk for the rest of my life." As did other ambitious young men without distinguished social backgrounds, he joined the army. After fighting in several bloody battles against the northern barbarians, he was promoted to captain.

Once, on a diplomatic mission, acting as an aide-de-camp, the captain accompanied a delegate named Guo Shun[2] with thirty imperial soldiers to visit the vast western territories. There were many countries with no definite political inclinations. This mission's main objective was to sign peace treaties with small and mid-sized realms to prevent them from collaborating with the powerful and belligerent northern barbarian tribes.

At the beginning of one meeting, a host king named Sang-Sun[3] received the Chinese delegates with manners and decorum. But after a few days, they were treated coldly. Noticing the change, the captain spoke to his superior.

"Your Highness, there is something fishy going on. I suspect that the king is meeting with our opponents, the northern barbarian diplomats. Otherwise, why would he suddenly change his attitude towards us? He is wondering which side he should make friends with. We have to deal with this potential crisis now before it is too late."

The delegate, who was only a mediocre diplomat, shook his head and made no comment. The captain, knowing his superior would do nothing, quickly excused himself and went back to his tent. He sought out and questioned a native servant, saying, "I know the northern representatives are here. I would like to get acquainted with them. Could you tell me where could I locate them?" The servant revealed all the details.

The captain, using a party as an excuse, assembled all of his assistants, about forty persons in total, and told them the situation. "Gentlemen, we leave our warm and cultivated country, traveling thousands of miles to these hot and uncivilized areas for what? Don't we want to get famous and prosperous someday? Now, the northern barbarian envoy, our biggest enemy, is negotiating with the host king, who consequently is treating us poorly. If the barbarians succeed, our mission fails. If the barbarians decide that our heads should be taken as proof of the reliability of their newly-built relationship, the host king will butcher us all. So what should we do?"

With despair the assistants looked at each other. No one knew what to do. "Please Sir, we are all at your service."

"Power and prosperity are earned, not given," the captain continued. "Our situation is critical. Time is against us. Our careers and future are at stake. The host is hesitating, trying to decide between us and the barbarians. We have to take advantage of his hesitation and attack the other delegates tonight. After we annihilate them, the king will be forced to endorse us."

Most of the assistants suggested that he should discuss the details with, or at least, as a courtesy, inform, their superior. "No need for that," the captain bluntly rebutted. "Heroic behavior can only be comprehended by a very few gifted champions. He is a civil servant, whose tunnel vision is always focused on regular procedure. How can we expect that he will approve this bold action, which is beyond his bird-brained comprehension? And if the king decides to ally himself with the barbarians tonight, our fates are sealed."

After hours of discussion, they developed a plan to storm the tents of the northern envoy. After this conference, the soldiers went back to their tents to oil swords, polish weapons and prepare torches. At midnight, they started the raid. One third of them set fire to enemy tents; another third, with arrows and bows, blocked the escape routes, and the rest of them attacked the diplomats who ran out of the tents. Over one hundred of the barbarians were burned to death and forty of them were killed in hand to hand fighting.

After the raid, with only a few of his warriors wounded, the captain reported this incident to his superior, who was astounded and terrified. "Your Highness," he comforted him, "if our government wants to punish the ringleader, I will personally take all the blame. On the other hand, if Our Majesty rewards us, Your Highness certainly deserve the highest honor." This calmed the delegate.

Learning of the attack, the host king was dumbfounded and sent his servants to chaperon the Chinese representatives to his palace. The delegate, sweating and useless, stood speechlessly while the captain presented the benefits of an alliance with his country, vigorously persuading the host to build a good relationship with China. After hours of debate, argument and persuasion, the king finally agreed to sign a peace treaty.

The Chinese emperor was pleased, and promoted the captain to emissary. According to diplomatic customs, the emperor intended to increase the number of the captain's entourage. But the captain politely declined. "I only need my old assistants. More people, especially in a crisis, will only be burdensome." He then undertook the duties of his new position by visiting the nomadic western territories.

His first stop was a western barbarian country called Yu-Tien[4] that had recently conquered one of its neighbor countries, and was welcoming the powerful northern barbarian envoy. The Chinese emissary was greeted in an aloof and unmannerly fashion.

In that country, superstitions dominated people's daily behavior and witchcraft prevailed. The supreme sorcerer, after a sacred ceremony, warned his master, "Our god is furious because you tolerate the Chinese delegates. He commands that you fetch the emissary's horse, butcher it and use its blood to appease our god's exasperation. Otherwise, he will curse your kingdom forever."

The king was worried, and immediately conveyed this holy decree to his unwelcome visitors. "Of course," the emissary said. "In fact, why don't you send the sorcerer himself to come and take my horse." The sorcerer duly arrived, and, dressed in his wild robes, arrogantly strode into the tent to collect the horse.

The emissary abruptly ordered his assistants to arrest him. After accusing him of sorcery, he directed his men to chop off this sorcerer's head and send it, with a letter of official reprimand, to the palace. Receiving the head and the letter, the king, who had already heard what this man had done a few months ago, slaughtered all of the northern delegates and their servants. The next day, pretending nothing happened, the king treated the Chinese emissary cordially and signed a peace treaty. Both parties neglected to mention any unpleasant episodes. The sorcerer's head and the bodies of those ill-fated northern delegates were buried in an obscure graveyard at midnight. The emissary, for winning more allies for China, was later promoted to general.

This is how an unknown clerk eventually became a high-ranking general. Due to braveness and cleverness, he mastered his own destiny, and his gallant behaviors became engraved forever in history.

In a period of turmoil, you may face difficulties and dilemmas. These are crises, turning points in your life. When encountering a crisis, treat it as a challenge, and with incentive and determination, try to convert this possible calamity into an opportunity. Be brave. A calculated risk is the only way to overcome a challenge and distinguish yourself from your peers.

To Deal With Mutinous Soldiers   *Tang Dynasty*
618 A.D. to 907 A.D.

How do you handle a group of powerful rebels? You can dispatch many soldiers to subdue them. However, it is very costly and time-consuming. On the other hand, with a scheme, you can trick them into submission, as a clever imperial aide did in the early ninth century A.D.

Once, the belligerent north-west barbarian tribes invaded China's borders. To support the threatened capital, the emperor Tang-Hsien[5] instructed a lord to return to his own domain and muster five thousand soldiers. The army was duly marshaled. However, the soldiers refused to travel to the capital and rebelled against their master. They assassinated the lord and occupied his realm. The central government, too busy with repelling the invaders, intentionally ignored the rebellion.

After a year of bloody war, the barbarians were finally driven back to their own territory. The emperor then turned his focus on those disloyal troops. Due to the turbulent circumstances, the mutinous soldiers were neither recognized as a regular national army, with proper salary, nor officially declared to be rebels, whom would be crushed. What should government do? The emperor held a secret imperial conference with many high-ranking generals and advisors and sought their opinions.

To uphold the reputation of the dynasty, all of the attendants unanimously agreed to denounce the soldiers as rebels and punish them. However, realizing the fatigued condition of their national guards, they weren't sure how to go about it.

"Your Majesty," an imperial aide Win Zau[6] said, "after a year-long campaign, our army is exhausted. How could they compete with the properly-fed and well-equipped rebels? Why bother to begin a civil war for seeking an eternal peace? And, if we lose, Your Majesty will be in great danger because we don't have soldiers to protect ourselves. Therefore, although our opponent is too powerful to conquer by force, a little cunning might solve this problem. I can personally manage them if Your Majesty will provide me with fifty elite imperial guards in plain clothes."

He then approached his master and murmured a scheme into his ear, which was duly approved. Several days later, the aide, as an imperial representative, visited those rebels, and presented them with expensive gifts and cattle. The rebels greeted the representative with skepticism. But after examining the gifts, the rebel officers felt a little relieved. Surprised by this unanticipated good fortune, they became boastful and sneered at this feeble-looking imperial delegate.

He announced, according to the emperor's decree, that those soldiers were to be treated as national guards due to their 'support' during the period of calamity. More presents, foodstuffs, and money were delivered in carriages to the rebels. After days of amenities, the delegate, who knew that he had buttered up the ringleaders and eliminated their suspicion, announced that he had to return to the capital in the next few days. The news greatly pleased those ringleaders, who thought that they would now freely control this area.

Using the ex-lord's mansion, the imperial representative threw a grandiose farewell party and invited all of the rebel leaders, who were delighted to attend. After all, what could he, a skinny bureaucrat, do to them?

In the foyer of the mansion they were greeted by a servant who asked them to hang their weapons in rope nooses, which had been set up in the foyer. The rebel leaders hung their weapons and then went inside and thoroughly enjoyed themselves. A delicious banquet was served, and fine wine was in generous supply.

Suddenly, at midnight, when most of the guests were drunk, the doors suddenly shut. The ropes with the weapons attached rose up to the ceiling, leaving the rebels' armaments dangling out of reach. The fifty imperial guards, fully armed, came out of hiding. The ringleaders were astonished and couldn't reach their swords. Drunk and unarmed, they fought fiercely with their bare hands, but the guards systematically massacred all of them.

In the morning, the delegate summoned all of the unarmed soldiers, whose weapons were locked in the armory, and publicly condemned the disloyalty of their leaders. He ordered them to disband. Leaderless, and seeing the fifty well-equipped imperial guards close at hand, the rebel army obeyed. All of the dismissed fighters became farmers, and dishonorable records were filed with the local authorities, who watched them closely and cautiously. A competent general was appointed to govern the region. From that day on, no one dared not to revolt against the government again. A potential civil war was shrewdly avoided.

A Clever Death

Warring States Period
475 B.C. to 221 B.C.

Can you believe this? A fatally wounded person lured his assassin to admit his crime. It happened over two thousand years ago during the Warring States period, when China was unfortunately divided into a handful of countries.

Due to a political dispute, a high-ranking government official hired an assassin to murder the prime minister, Mr. Sue Chin.[7] The plot was successful and the assassin vanished. Martial law was proclaimed and high bounty offered for the murderer.

On his death bed, the fatally wounded prime minister urged the king Chi-Min[8] to take part in a ploy to catch the criminal.

"Your Majesty, after I die, please declare that I am a foreign agent, quarter my body, toss it, piece by piece, into the crowded boulevards, and offer to generously reward the conspirators, who will certainly disclose their 'heroic behavior.' Then, Your Majesty can avenge my death." The king agreed with the plan.

Martial law was discontinued when new pieces of 'evidence' were discovered that indicated that the ex-prime minister was actually a traitor. The king declared that the bounty had now became an award. A few days later, the high-ranking official and the assassin, who heard this good news and promptly came out of hiding, cheerfully and proudly revealed their intrigue and requested the award. But much to their dismay, they were arrested, put on trial, and sentenced to death. The king then announced the truth, ordered his servants to collect the pieces of the ex-prime minister's body, sew them up, place them in a costly coffin, and bury the body in a well-furnished grave with honor and decorum.

The prime minister was quite clever. After his death, he used his flesh and bones to catch his killer. He thoroughly comprehended one of the human's basic inclinations: avoid punishment and pursue reward. By merely calling a bounty a reward, those two lawbreakers swarmed to their destiny.

An Untrained Mayor

Three Kingdoms Period
220 A.D. to 280 A.D.

In the old days, the imperial government often selected educated gentlemen to be mayors if they had passed imperial examinations or received a recommendation from the local authority. However, in times of political turbulence, military personnel, due to their exceptional battlefield merits, would be appointed mayor instead. Though competent commanders, these men were often looked down upon as ignorant and unschooled by their classically-educated counterparts, and oftentimes friction would develop. An episode from the chaotic Three Kingdoms Period demonstrated how one military man proved he could match wits with his educated aides.

A lieutenant colonel Hwang Gai,[9] in the country Wu, which occupied most part of Southern China, was commissioned to be a mayor in a small city. The local officials of that city, who were well-educated, were notorious for their arrogance toward their superiors. They always looked down on and rarely paid any respect to their chief executive. How can one, especially a poorly-educated military man, cope with those snobs who not only had more schooling, but had resided in the area for generations and knew every inch of the city?

Upon receiving the mayorship, this lieutenant colonel immediately assembled all of his egotistical subordinates and suggested that they elect two deputy mayors among themselves. This order was half-heartedly carried out. Two officials were chosen and skeptically accepted their new promotions. A few days later, the newly-appointed mayor issued a bulletin. It stated: "Although I am the mayor, you all know that I am a military person. Obtaining this position because of my skill on the battlefield, I, frankly speaking, know nothing about ruling people. There are highwaymen harassing some parts of my domain, which I will personally deal with. The two deputy mayors can take care of local matters for me. They can sign any documents on my behalf. However, if they abuse this privilege, they will be punished according to the book of laws."

Reading this unconventional announcement, those subordinates, at the beginning, paid attention to their behavior. However, due to lack of supervision and contempt for their undereducated superior, they gradually slackened their discretion and started to mishandle lawsuits and manipulate local affairs for their own gain. "After all, who gives a damn about that illiterate soldier anyway?" they frequently remarked behind his back.

The mayor however, had secretly dispatched his servants to monitor the two deputies and collect evidence of any wrongdoing. In a few weeks, possessing some solid evidence of inappropriate behavior, the shrewd mayor gathered all of his subordinates together and presented the evidence. Shocked, with great embarrassment, the deputies knelt and begged for mercy. "Oh no. Not this time." the master sternly remarked. "I did warn you in writing. Everybody knew it."

The two deputy mayors were charged with accepting bribes, embezzling, and incompetence. Their crimes were proven beyond doubt. According to the law, they were sentenced to death and promptly executed. Amazed by this severe turn of events, the other subordinates trembled. Two new deputy mayors were elected to handle local matters. With great reluctance, they accepted the positions, and then did their best to improve the administration. No one dared to tangle with the "illiterate solider" ever again.

A Yes Man
Ming Dynasty
1368 A.D. to 1644 A.D.

How can you discover the moral inclinations of your aides? An ordinary supervisor may clandestinely dispatch someone to observe them. Or, he will evaluate his subordinates' daily activities all by himself. But they for sure will not reveal any incompetence or infidelity right in front of their superior. However, with a simple scheme, you can get them to show you their genuine character in no time, as did a county mayor long ago.

A government official named Kwon Zon[10] was assigned to a county position. Upon receiving his position as mayor, he began to review complaints and lawsuits. Strangely enough, he spent no more than two minutes on each case, no matter how complex it was. Briefly browsing through each case, he immediately approved and endorsed it with his official seal. Observing this, his subordinates were thrilled since they were the ones who had prepared the cases.

"What a simpleton!" they privately sneered. Without his interference, they were the real power in the county. They gradually tangled with the laws and bent rules for their personal gain. The newly appointed county mayor seemed not to care and continued to blindly endorse every case.

This peculiar practice had lasted over a month. Then one day he assembled all of his aides and showed them a written proclamation from the emperor. It stated that the mayor had the liberty to sentence and execute any mid-level government officials without confirmation from the palace. It was a privilege for very few high-ranking officials. All the attendants were more puzzled than surprised and did not utter a word of comment.

After this brief announcement, the mayor cited a case in which one of his aides cheated on a lawsuit and received handsome bribes from defendants. With amazement, the alleged subordinate embarrassingly admitted his misdeed, expecting to receive a pardon. Without any hesitation, the county mayor calmly ordered his muscular bodyguards to press the offender on the ground and spank him to death, which was the strictest interpretation of the punishment. He then quoted another violation and executed the law-breaker in a similar fashion. In less than three hours, he did away with six of his most corrupt aides. The others were astounded, trembling and shuddering, and nervously looked at this cruel scene with despair.

The mayor directed his servants to place those bodies in the most crowded market, with their crimes clearly written on a nearby board. The other subordinates, who violated the laws in less extreme ways, were deliberately overlooked and allowed to go home. After that event, they dared not to abuse their superior's trust anymore.

As a famous military strategist once remarked, "Thoroughly know yourself and your enemy, you will never lose a single battle." As a newcomer, how can you understand your subordinates? Play dumb. Let them show their true personalities. Then, severely discipline the worst offenders. The others will be more than happy to fall into the line and become law-abiding persons again.

CHAPTER TWELVE

Good Judgment

To Straighten Out the Mess

Northern Wei Dynasty
534 A.D. to 550 A.D.

How do you handle a complicated task that is of trivial importance? This interesting event happened in the Northern Wei dynasty, a period of political chaos and economic devastation in which China was unfortunately in disunity.

A powerful nobleman named Gao Hwan[1] wanted to test his sons' crisis-management skills. One day, he gave each of the sons some knotted and tangled silk strings and demanded they straighten them out.

All of the sons mindfully tried to untangle the mess, except one son, Gao Yan.[2] After watching his brothers fumble and tug at the knotted strings, he drew his sword and chopped the bundles into little pieces. His brothers were amazed and dumbfounded, and his father questioned him about this unusual behavior.

"It is simple," the dauntless son answered. "Which one is more important—my time or resolving this mess? What is the trade-off for the loss of the former and the gain of the later? Whatever is too complicated to be resolved within a reasonable amount of time is a total waste and not worth my attention. To chop it up and throw it away, with little loss, I think, is the most effective method in dealing with such a problem."

The nobleman was greatly pleased with his son's actions. After a few years, this son dethroned the emperor and crowned himself.

People often focus on resolving a problem and forget the costs of the procedure. As a result, they frequently spend their precious time on trivialities for pitiable gain. Time, one of the most valuable and also overlooked commodities, should always be calculated when handling a dilemma. Whoever treasures it will get the most out of life.

Build a Castle

Northern Sung Dynasty
960 A.D. to 1127 A.D.

Should you be discouraged by your opponents' protest? On the contrary, you should be encouraged by it. Why is that? This episode will explain.

General Chiang Jai[3] suggested to his commander, Wong Sue,[4] that they should build a castle on a certain strategically important border area, which, regardless of many colleagues' and subordinates' objections, was permitted. So the general started the construction. But before completing this stronghold, the northern barbarians attacked. They defeated the general's guards, massacred most of the workers, ravaged the materials and burned down the half-finished castle.

The general, who was wounded, went back and reported this misfortune to his superior, and also offered his resignation. Some of the commander's aides, who had opposed this project from the beginning, advised their superior to court-martial the general for this humiliating loss.

"Of course not," the commander laughed heartedly and commented, "why should I ruin one of my most competent and reliable generals' career to please my rival? To tell you the truth, at the beginning, I was skeptical about the significance of this fortress and hesitantly approved this project. Now, from this setback, I realize that our enemy is alarmed by its existence. I am thoroughly convinced of its importance and he shall have my full support on rebuilding it."

He kindly consoled the dejected general and immediately sent him back with more troops, workers, and construction materials. The commander's aide-de-camp, Di Chin,[5] said "This attack is only a warning. Next time the northern barbarians will initiate a full-scale invasion to destroy this castle. I'm afraid that the pigheaded and foolhardy general might lose his life for it."

"It might be," the commander remarked. "However, it is our enemy's decision. My main concern is whether we should or should not build this fortress and who will benefit from it? Learning from this assault, I believe the barbarians are uncomfortable about, or even terrified of, the existence of this castle, which means that we are in the right direction. We have to continue and finish it on the double. If they attack us again, you will reinforce them. If you can't drive them back, I will personally bring the garrison guards and every single able man to help you. We should not budge an inch on this fundamentally important issue." The castle eventually finished without any interference from the unfriendly northern neighbors.

Kill the Delegate

Eastern Han Dynasty
25 A.D. to 220 A.D.

In a military deadlock, how could you tilt the balance to your advantage? This story, which took place during the Eastern Han dynasty, presents one solution.

In the early first century, a period of political disorder and massive destruction, the new emperor Han-Gwon Wu,[6] dispatched some of his most capable generals to crush a powerful rebel army. Their troops confronted each other. After several bloody battles, the imperial army defeated the rebels and eventually besieged the enemy's capital, where there were over a hundred thousand rebels.

The conflict became a deadlock. The attackers could not conquer this city nor could the defenders repel them. Time helped no one. Both sides suffered a shortage of foodstuffs, medicine and clothes, and morale was rock bottom. Desertion and insubordination were frequent. Mutiny was expected at any moment.

The leaders of the two armies finally agreed to negotiate. Knowing that, the emperor sent one his ablest generals, Ko Shuen,[7] as his representative. The rebel leader Gao Guen,[8] sent his chief of staff, a man named Hwanfu Win[9]—his smartest and most trusted aide—to meet with the imperial agent.

They met. The rebel delegate was aloof and arrogant, and talks were abruptly discontinued. The imperial agent wanted to kill the rebel delegate, a dishonorable act that went against all of the official customs, and was vigorously opposed by all the emperor's assistants.

But the general wouldn't listen. He ordered his bodyguards to arrest and kill the snobbish delegate, but spare the delegate's aide. The aide, carrying a letter which indicated that the whole incident was caused by the delegate's non-cooperative attitude, was chaperoned to the entrance of the besieged city. This letter also served as an ultimatum—unconditional surrender within two days or full-scale attack and massacre. The next day, the rebel ring-leader gave in.

Every aide and colleague came to congratulate the general and asked the same question. "After slaughtering the enemy's most trustworthy chief of staff, why did they give up the fight? Don't they want revenge?"

"Of course they do," he casually commented. "But they are not able to. The delegate was too insolent, which indicated that they didn't intend to give themselves up at all. As a shrewd observer, he was here to investigate our mil-itary strength and soldiers' morale. A competent foe is the greatest threat to our success. His existence was counter-productive. If I spared his life, his return would encourage the rebels, and they would renew the fighting with us, which would be a disadvantage or even a disaster for us. I decided I must terminate him, the best leader our opponent has, to crush their morale. Without him, the rebel leader was mentally hopeless, and saw no choice but to surrender."

As a famous military strategist once remarked, "To smash the rival's morale is the foremost objective in winning a conflict."

Push the Law All the Way   *Warring States Period, 475 B.C. to 221 B.C.*

This episode happened in the turbulent Warring States period, when China was unfortunately divided into a handful of countries.

A slave escaped from his native state and sought refuge in a neighboring country. The slave's owner, Lord Wei,[10] was the lord of the state. He offered a reward of fifty ounces of pure gold, which was much more than the cost of that slave, to get that fugitive back.

The king of the country to which the slave fled rejected that price and refused to hand him over. The lord then decided to offer a mid-sized town in exchange for that slave.

"Your Lordship, is the fugitive worth such high a price?" one of his min-isters cautiously advised.

"You must look at the big picture," the master remarked. "To successful-ly rule a state, I must not pay too much attention to pennies and dimes.

Instead, I have to set the rules straight. Otherwise, my people will neither respect me nor follow the laws faithfully. As a result, my country will become disorganized and eventually be destroyed. When someone challenges my authority, I must punish him at all costs to let others learn a valuable lesson — don't mess with your master. Not only will my people never break a rule, they will respect me for the serious manner in which I uphold the law. Therefore, giving away a town to accomplish that goal is very inexpensive."

What a far-sighted ruler! He knew that to successfully govern his people he must have their respect. As an old saying goes, "With people's support, you will be prosperous. Without their endorsement, you will be ruined."

Find Your Edge

Eastern Han Dynasty
25 A.D. to 220 A.D.

People often mistakenly believe that an army with an overwhelming number of soldiers will easily claim victory. Please read history carefully. It is not always so. There was a very famous battle in 208 A.D. that illustrates my point.

After destroying a handful of warlords in the north, the prime minister Tsaur Tsau[11] intended to subdue Lord Sung Chuan,[12] whose domain was in the south. Through a letter, the prime minister declared that he would march eight hundred thousand well-equipped soldiers to 'hunt' in the southern territory if the lord were foolish enough to refuse surrendering all of his army.

Shocked, the southern lord showed the letter to all his ministers. After understanding the threat, they were profoundly depressed. The number of their troops was less than one-tenth of the enemy's. How could they have any chance of coping with them? The palace became deathly quiet.

After brief amenities, Jang Zou,[13] a high-ranking official who had assisted the master's elder brother to establish this realm and was the single most prestigious person in the region, woefully expressed his opinion.

"Why should we struggle for a hopeless cause? We must send a team of delegates to negotiate our surrender, and try to get the best terms that we can out of this hazardous situation." Most of the attendants agreed with him. However, one minister named Lu Shu[14] vigorously opposed this plan. He advised the lord to summon a senior general named Chou Yu,[15] who was training ships on a lake, to discuss this matter. The master agreed.

In a few days, General Chou Yu, who was one of the most capable military strategists of his time, returned. At a planning conference among all the high-ranking officials and senior generals, he objectively presented his analysis of the strengths and weaknesses of both sides.

"The invader kidnaps Our Majesty. Using our emperor's name, he tries to unify the whole country for his own offspring. He is nothing but a shameless and crafty thief. Why should we seek peace with the wicked while we are on the side of justice? Allow me to evaluate our human resources and military strengths."

All the attendants, who were mostly in their late fifties, were fascinated by the boldness and intelligence of this young commander, who was in his mid-thirties. After a brief pause, he continued. "The Yangtze river divides China into two, the North and the South. Due to distinct climates, the people have different life-styles and customs. They eat wheat and us, rice. Our opponents are very experienced in cavalry warfare. Our specialty is naval battles. Because of these distinctions, I believe we can successfully outmaneuver our foes if we prepare ourselves properly. Their cavalry, which are their best troops, will become clumsy and inefficient on our river-riddled plains. Our navy certainly has the advantage of locality. Please give me fifty thousand soldiers, and I will finish the job."

The lord was deeply impressed and commissioned the general to be the supreme commander of this battle. The northern invaders' main force, which had to be transported by hundreds of boats, was attacked by the southerners, who were adept at fighting on the wide surface of the Yangtze. Many enemy boats were set afire. Encountering devastating ambushes and suffering many casualties, the remaining northern army retreated in disarray. The invasion failed miserably. The victory secured the political independence of this southern domain for another 72 years.

Don't be afraid of powerful enemies. Study them carefully and you will find a way to exploit their weaknesses and your advantages. Be your own master. After all, you could hardly accomplish anything under another's mercy.

Face the Trouble
Northern Sung Dynasty
960 A.D. to 1127 A.D.

Picture this: you are attacked by a tiger. Can you feed that ferocious animal your arm and naively expect that he will leave the rest of your body alone? Of course not. The same idea can be applied to politics and war, as shown by an event from the Northern Sung dynasty.

The northeastern barbarian tribes mobilized all of their armies and invaded China. The border troops couldn't stop their overwhelming aggression and gradually retreated. In one day, five alarming messages were delivered to the imperial palace, urging Emperor Sung-Chen[16] to reinforce those armies as soon as possible.

The emperor was deeply troubled. He summoned the prime minister Kwo Joen[17] to his private chambers and discussed this pressing matter. After brief amenities, the cool-headed prime minister suggested that the emperor should personally visit the battlefied.

"Are you out of your mind?" shouted the emperor. Amazed by this bold recommendation, the master, whose face instantly turned pale, rebuked his advisor. "Why should I go north and risk my own life over those barbarians? Can't I just send a few capable generals to handle it for me?"

"I am afraid that is not possible." answered the prime minister calmly. "Our enemy is deadly serious. They are betting all of their chips in this wild game. We must counter them with nothing less than the very best. All of the country belongs to Your Majesty. With persistence and boldness, Your Majesty will preserve all of it. On the other hand, if we yield an inch of land, we may never regain it. How much territory can Your Majesty afford to give away?"

Considering it for a long while, the master agreed to lead the army himself. The next day however, at an imperial conference, many officials suggested otherwise. One senior minister named Wong Chin-Zou[18] advised relocating the capital city to southern China. Chen Yau-Yue,[19] another high-ranking official, advocated moving the government to a certain location in the southeastern area of the country. The emperor, who did not want to go near the battle, began to waver. He said he would like to seriously evaluate those two possibilities.

"Poppycock!" shouted the prime minister at the two officials. "Do you want to be charged with treason for suggesting such things?" He turned to face the emperor. "Will Your Majesty be pleased to hold a half or even a quarter of our empire? Why should we voluntarily retreat to those distant areas? Once we shy away from the aggressor, our morale will be shattered forever. Then, where can Your Majesty go and find shelter? In this period of a great danger we must move forward to bravely face the challenge. Otherwise, our fates will be sealed for certain by our cowardice."

With anxiety and reluctance, the master accepted his viewpoint and ordered his servants to announce that he would lead an army. In less than a week, hearing that announcement, many commanders and generals zealously advanced their troops to accompany their master. When the emperor's flag was detected on a battlefield, the soldiers roared with excitement. It became their guiding star. Believing that their godlike emperor indeed cherished them, the soldiers did their best to defend their homeland. After a few bloody military engagements, the enemy's invasion was halted. Foreseeing the hopelessness of the war, the northern invaders sought peace. Soon they signed a treaty with China.

In a life-and-death situation, when your strength is equal to the enemy's, you must dauntlessly confront the enemy head-on. If you flinch from the crisis, you will be swept into oblivion by the tide of events. As master of your fate, you must face the challenge directly.

Show Your Charisma

Tang Dynasty
618 A.D. to 907 A.D.

In periods of political chaos, poorly-disciplined soldiers often took the law into their own hands and frequently disturbed law-abiding citizens. If martial law were declared, servicemen were directly under their commander's supervision, and local authorities could not interfere with their activities, whether legal or illegal. If you were a mayor, how would you deal with military hoodlums?

During a bloody civil war, many ill-mannered soldiers, stationed in a city in central China, often quarreled and sometimes even fought with local peddlers. The citizens were afraid of the unruly soldiers, and stayed in their houses, hoping to be left alone. Once, due to a trivial dispute, some soldiers beat a tavern owner to death. This atrocity was immediately reported to the local authority.

The county mayor, Guo Si[20] was very angry and instantly dispatched two squads of marshals to round up the murderous soldiers. After a speedy trial, he ordered his men to behead them all in the most crowded market. Their crime was written on a nearby official bulletin board and their heads were hung on the main gate as a warning to others.

But his infringement of military jurisdiction caused a great commotion in the barracks. Indignant soldiers put on their armor, took out weapons and started to oil them, and prepared to lynch that 'arrogant' mayor.

This was reported to the mayor, who immediately visited the barracks and casually remarked, "Why bother to look for me? I am here with my head."

With amazement the soldiers stared at this bold official, who calmly called on the headquarters. Overhearing the excitement, the general came out, cordially greeted the mayor, and invited him in his tent. After brief amenities, the visitor said "Your father is the most powerful general in our dynasty. But look at yourself. Do you not feel a little shameful, allowing your soldiers to assault harmless civilians? Do you want to damage your father's reputation?"

The mayor then told him of the offense and his resolution. With surprise, the general apologized for those misdeeds and commanded his aide-de-camp to stop the other soldiers' preparations for mayhem. That order was executed with efficiency.

"It is too late for me to travel back to the city," the mayor said. "Can I have my dinner here?" The general promptly agreed. Learning that, the soldiers were astounded by his braveness. By all means, there were many hot-tempered servicemen would love to kill him in revenge for their dead compatriots. After the meal, the mayor requested to stay the night, which was mannerly granted. Astonished by his fearless conduct, the general privately dispatched his most trusted bodyguards to protect this visitor all night. The next morning, the mayor safely left the camp. The soldiers admired him for his braveness and dared not disturb local tranquillity again.

Detecting an upcoming difficulty, people often bury their heads in the sand and hope that trouble will pass them by. By not confronting the problem, they unwisely leave themselves at the mercy of circumstance.

Be active instead. Your supreme enemy is your own doubt and hesitation. Take fate into your own hands. Show your charisma to your opponents. You can convince them, with proper justification, of the rightness of your actions. At the very least, they will for sure admire your courage.

By Persuasion

Northern Sung Dynasty
1127 A.D. to 1279 A.D.

Nobody wants trouble. When confronted with a problem, you may be able to talk your way out of it if you keep this in mind—that the people who initiate the conflict most likely don't want to be in that situation either. Find out the real cause of the disturbance and you may avoid serious trouble. A hair-raising incident that illustrates my point occurred in the Northern Sung dynasty.

A government official named Con Yuon[21] was assigned to a border city. After only three days as mayor, he surprisingly discovered that all of his soldiers and police were gone. They had been dispatched to handle a revolt in another corner of the province. Worse than that, the aborigines, who were fully armed with swords and spears, surrounded the city and were preparing to attack.

The mayor immediately had an urgent conference with his subordinates. They all suggested bolting the gates and sending letters to neighboring cites, asking for military assistance.

"If we are lucky enough, we can hold them at bay until the rescuers arrive," some of them estimated. There was no time to assemble and train local citizens to protect this city.

"We must send a delegate to find out their problem first," said the mayor. "Otherwise, regardless of the resolution, we will never know the cause of the uprising."

"What a lunatic!" his subordinates privately sneered. Out loud they said "How could we possibly approach those barbarians with their oiled swords and sharpened spears? And may we ask who will have the honor to meet with those ferocious rebels?" None of them wanted to receive this fatal assignment.

Without any hesitation, the mayor volunteered himself. Although his subordinates pleaded with the mayor not to go, their protest was merely a formality. They were only too happy to let the mayor put his own neck on the chopping block.

Accompanied by two aged servants, the mayor appeared at the city gates, which immediately caused a commotion. The armed natives had expected to be met by a few hundred well-armed soldiers. Instead, a solitary man rode out to meet them.

After brief amenities to the invaders, the rider said, "I am the new mayor of this city. I would like to discuss with your leader why you threaten the city. Please, guide me to your headquarters." Surprised by this request and by he mayor's polite demeanor, the natives escorted him to their village. While on their way to the village, the mayor's two servants made excuses and snuck away, which meant that one of the barbarian warriors had to hold the horse's reins for him.

When they arrived at the village, the barbarian chief came out to meet the mayor. The mayor got down off of his horse and said "I am your superior. Traditionally, you must call on me first."

He then strode into a tent and sat on a bed, waiting. With astonishment, the barbarian leader went in to 'call' on the mayor. After formal amenities, the mayor asked the reason for their untimely 'hunting.' The natives vigorously complained about the corruption of the last mayor and told of many injustices that they had suffered. Due to over-taxation and other maltreatment, they didn't have sufficient food and cattle to endure the coming winter.

Mindfully listening to their protest, the mayor considered it for a moment and said "I do understand your outrage and sympathize with your suffering. My predecessor has done wrong to you all. I apologize for him. Being your new superior, I am responsible for you. You can send someone with me tomorrow to fetch cattle and supplies. For now, it is rather late for me to return to the city. I will stay here for the night."

The natives admired this mayor for his brazenness and deeply appreciated him for his thoughtfulness. The next morning, the mayor, with a company of natives, went back to the city. Observing their approach, his subordinates wrongfully believed that their superior was leading the rebels to assail the city.

After an exchange of words, they agreed to allow him to come in alone. In a few hours, the mayor collected a hundred tons of rice, vegetables, and cattle. He personally supervised the delivery. Receiving these goods, the natives were thankful for his kindness, and loudly swore their loyalty to him.

People, as well as countries, are often in conflict. The clumsiest way to settle the matter is a fist fight between people or a war between nations. Physical confrontations are costly and ineffective, and generally solve nothing at all. Try to learn your opponent's viewpoint. Communicate and compromise until you can reach an acceptable outcome. After all, any fool can start a fight. To resolve a conflict without violence is an art, and a sign of wisdom.

NOTES

I. SUPREME WISDOM
Chapter 1 — Look at the Whole Picture

1. King Yang-Jau, "the Bright," 燕昭王 Reign 311-279 B.C.
2. Guo Wai, 郭隗
3. Tzy Gon, 子貢 520 B.C.-?
4. Bin Jyi. 丙吉 ?-55 B.C.
5. Emperor Tang-Kao, "the Magnificent," 唐高宗 Reign 650-683 A.D.
6. Wai Yuan-Jong, 魏元忠
7. Leou Bei, 柳玭
8. Hsiao Ho, 蕭何 ?-193 B.C.
9. Lin Shan-Lu, 藺相如
10. Lian Poo, 廉頗
11. Lee Yuan, Emperor Tang-Kao, "the Great," 唐高祖李淵 Reign 618-626 A.D.
12. Lord Meng-Ch'ang, 孟嘗君
13. Feng Shuan, 馮煖
14. Tai-Gong-Wan, "The Grandpa Wan," 太公望
15. Hwa Shi, 華士

Chapter 2 — Avoid Future Problems

1. Emperor Tang-Teh, "the Decent," 唐德宗 Reign 780-784 A.D.
2. Bai Chi, 白起 ?-257 B.C.
3. Lee Mee, 李泌 722-789 A.D.
4. Emperor Sung-Kao "the Eminent," 宋高宗 Reign 1127-1162 A.D.
5. Chau Din, 趙鼎 1085-1147 A.D.
6. Chern Shen-Jee, 陳升之 1011-1079 A.D.
7. Wong Dan, 王旦 957-1017 A.D.
8. Lee Hang, 李沆 947-1004 A.D.
9. Lord Gin-Li "the Hot-blood," 晉厲公 Reign 580-573 B.C.
10. Fan Shieh, 范燮
11. Emperor Tang-Teh "the Decent," 唐德宗 Reign 780-804 A.D.
12. Lee Chan, 李晟 727-793 A.D.
13. Gonsong Yee, 公孫儀
14. Ho Zan, 何真
15. Wong Chen, 王成
16. Emperor Sung-Shen "the Concentrated," 宋神宗 Reign 1068-1085 A.D.
17. Syma Guang, 司馬光 1019-1086 A.D.

Chapter 3 — Keep It Simple and Clear

1. Tang-Wen, "the Cultivated," 唐文宗 Reign 826-840 A.D.
2. Emperor Han-Kuan-Wu, "the Militant," 漢光武帝 Reign 25-57 A.D.
3. Hsiao Dau-Chen, 蕭道成 427-482 A.D.
4. Lee Gi, 李及
5. Fan Fon, 范諷

6. Liu Shun-Chin, 劉舜卿
7. Lee Yun-Jer, 李允則
8. Win Yan-Bo, 文彦博 1006-1097 A.D.
9. Lee Fong, 李封
10. Shiue Charng-Ru, 薛長孺
11. Guo Tzy-Yi, 郭子儀 697-781 A.D.
12. Peir Shiuh, 裴婿

Chapter 4 — Wedge Your Way In

1. Ju Shen-Fay, 朱勝非
2. Emperor Sung-Kao, "the Eminent," 宋高宗 Reign 1127-1162 A.D.
3. Emperor Han-Wu, "the Militant," 漢武帝 Reign 140-87 B.C.
4. Zufu Yan, 主父偃 ?-126 B.C.
5. Emperor Tang-Hsuan, "the Abstruse," 唐玄宗 Reign 712-755 A.D.
6. Peir Gwn-Tin, 裴光庭 675-732 A.D.
7. Tang-Teh, "the Decent," 唐德宗 Reign 780-804 A.D.
8. Tsuei Yo-Fu, 崔祐甫 721-780 A.D.
9. Tsaur Bin, 曹彬 931-999 A.D.
10. Emperor L. Chou-Shih, 後周世宗 Reign 954-958 A.D.
11. Lee Shan, 李賢 1408-1466 A.D.
12. Emperor Ming-Wu, "the Militant," 明武宗 Reign 1506-1521 A.D.
13. Jean Bin, 江彬
14. Young Tin-Ho, 楊廷和 1459-1529 A.D.
15. Wong Choung, 王瓊
16. Emperor Sung-Ying, "the Bright," 宋英宗 Reign 1064-1067 A.D.
17. Han Chi, 韓琦 1008-1075 A.D.

II. SAGACIOUS WISDOM
Chapter 5 — Keen Perception

1. Emperor Shang-Jow, "the Cruel," 商紂王 Reign 1154?-1122? B.C.
2. Gee Tzy, 箕子
3. Emperor Chou-Wu, "the Militant," 周武王
4. Chou-Gong "the old man Chou," 周公
5. Tzy Gon, 子貢 520 B.C.-?
6. Lord Chi-Huan, 齊桓公 685-643 B.C.
7. Goan Jong, 管仲 ?-645 B.C.
8. Yee Ya, 易牙
9. Sue Dau, 豎刀
10. Chan Ze-Wu, 常之巫
11. Chi Fon, 啟方
12. Tien Chen-Tzy, 田成子
13. Shyi Shih-Mi, 隰斯彌
14. Emperor Sung-Kao, "the Eminent," 宋高宗 Reign 1127-1162 A.D.
15. Yueh Fei, 岳飛 1103-1142 A.D.
16. Kin Wu-Jwu, 金兀朮 ?-1148 A.D.
17. Wong Mang, 王莽 45 B.C.-23 A.D.
18. Ju-Tzy-Ying, "the Baby Child," 孺子嬰 Reign 6-8 A.D.
19. Zen-Win-Gon, 任文公
20. Tsay Gin, 蔡京 1047-1126 A.D.
21. Zou Win, 朱溫 852-912 A.D.

22. Lee Ker-Yuon, 李克用 856-924 A.D.
23. Emperor Tang-Chao, "the Luminous," 唐昭宗 Reign 889-903 A.D.
24. Wan Er, 萬二
25. Emperor Ming-Tai, "the Grand Progenitor," 明太祖 Reign 1368-1398 A.D.

Chapter 6 — Reckon and Calculate

1. Gin Win-Tzy, 晉文子
2. Miow Shan, 繆賢
3. Lin Shan-Lu, 藺相如
4. Yau Czon, 姚崇 650-721 A.D.
5. Jang Shuo, 張說 667-730 A.D.
6. Jang Chuan, 張勤
7. Dachi Bau-Huei, 達奚抱暉
8. Emperor Tang-Teh, "the Decent," 唐德宗 Reign 780-804 A.D.
9. Lee Mi, 李泌 722-789 A.D.
10. Woei Shiaw-Kuan, 韋孝寬 509-580 A.D.
11. Yau Yueh, 姚岳
12. Emperor Han-Hsien, "the Soft," 漢獻帝 Reign 190-220 A.D.
13. Tsaur Tsau, 曹操 155-220 A.D.
14. Yuan Shau, 袁紹 ?-202 A.D.
15. Gonsun Kan, 公孫康
16. Lu Shiun, 陸遜 183-245 A.D.
17. Zuger Keh, 諸葛恪 203-253 A.D.

Chapter 7 — Analyze the Doubtful

1. Tsiao Ker-Min, 曹克明
2. Emperor Han-Chao, "the Bright," 漢昭帝 Reign 923-933 A.D.
3. Liu Dan, King Yan, 燕王劉旦
4. Huoh Gwan, 霍光 ?-68 B.C.
5. Chau Yuan-Jo, 趙元佐
6. Emperor Sung-Tai "the Established," 宋太祖 Reign 976-997 A.D.
7. Kwo Joen, 寇準 961-1022 A.D.
8. Shiman Bau, 西門豹
9. Emperor L. Tang-Min, "the Bright," 後唐明宗 Reign 923-933 A.D.
10. Chau Fon, 趙鳳 ?-935 A.D.
11. Lin Jiun, 林俊 1452-1527 A.D.
12. Hwan Jan, 黃震

Chapter 8 — Orchestrate the Complexes

1. Chorng Shyh-Herng, 種世衡
2. Emperor Ming-Hsien, "the Honest," 明憲宗 Reign 1465-1487 A.D.
3. Yau Kwei, 姚夔 1414-1473 A.D.
4. Jo Zen, 周忱 1381-1453 A.D.
5. Chao Bian, 趙抃 1008-1084 A.D.
6. Woei Shiaw-Kuan, 韋孝寬 509-580 A.D.
7. Yuwin Tai, 宇文泰 507-556 A.D.
8. Fan Chwen-Zan, 范純仁 1027-1101 A.D.
9. Jang Shiu, 張需

III OBSERVANT WISDOM
Chapter 9 — Sharp and Penetrating

1. Lee Gin, 李靖 571-649 A.D.
2. Emperor Tang-Gau, "the Great," 唐高祖 Reign 618-627 A.D.
3. Jang Chi-Shan, 張齊賢 943-1014 A.D.
4. Hwan Ba, 黃霸
5. Fan Tai, 范邰
6. Ju Kai, 朱鎧
7. Yin Yuen-Gi, 殷雲霽
8. Zou Yu, 周紆
9. Jang Jeu, 張舉
10. Jang Chau, 張潮
11. Lee Main, 李勉 717-788 A.D.
12. Yuan Ze, 袁滋
13. Lee Huai, 李惠

Chapter 10 — Expose the Vicious

1. Yuen Gian, 元絳 1009-1083 A.D.
2. Chau Kwan-Han, 趙廣漢 ?-65 B.C.
3. Jang Shau-Sher, 張小舍
4. Shan Min-Zon, 向敏中 949-1020 A.D.
5. Hu Gi-Zon, 胡汲仲
6. Young Fen-Chuen, 楊逢春
7. Liu Zon-Gwai, 劉宗龜
8. Mulon Yan-Chau, 慕容彥超

IV DAUNTLESS INTELLIGENCE
Chapter 11 — Brave and Bold

1. Ban Chau, 班超 32-102 A.D.
2. Guo Shun, 郭恂
3. Sang-Sun, 鄯善王
4. Yu-Tien, 于闐國
5. Emperor Tang-Hsien, "the Intelligent," 唐憲宗 Reign 806-820 A.D.
6. Win Zau, 溫照 766-835 A.D.
7. Sue Chin, 蘇秦
8. King Chi-Min, 齊湣王 Reign 342-324 B.C.
9. Hwang Gai, 黃蓋
10. Kwon Zon, 況鍾

Chapter 12 — Good Judgment

1. Gao Hwan, 高歡 496-547 A.D.
2. Gao Yan, 高洋 529-559 A.D.
3. Chiang Jai, 蔣偕
4. Wong Sue, 王素 1007-1073 A.D.
5. Di Chin, 狄青 1008-1057 A.D.
6. Emperor Han-Gwon-Wu, "the Great," 漢光武帝 Reign 25-57 A.D.
7. Ko Shuen, 寇恂 ?-36 A.D.
8. Gao Guen, 高峻
9. Hwanfu Win, 皇甫文

10. Lord Wei, 衞嗣君 Reign 324-283 B.C.
11. Tsaur Tsau, 曹操 155-220 A.D.
12. Sung Chuan, 孫權 182-252 A.D.
13. Jang Zou, 張昭 156-236 A.D.
14. Lu Shu, 魯肅 172-217 A.D.
15. Chou Yu, 周瑜 175-210 A.D.
16. Emperor Sung-Chen, "the Kind," 宋真宗 Reign 1023-1065 A.D.
17. Kwo Joen, 寇準 961-1022 A.D.
18. Wong Chin-Zou, 王欽若 962-1025 A.D.
19. Chen Yau-Yue, 陳堯叟
20. Guo Si, 郭晞
21. Con Yuon, 孔鏞

About the Editor

Feng, Mon-Lon (1574–1646 A.D.) was a low-level civil servant during the last years of the Ming dynasty (1368–1644 A.D.) A student of political intrigue, he compiled and edited many short stories. In 1626, selecting primarily from well-known historical events, he assembled a work of 28 volumes, with over 830 stories, in only two months. The stories in this book come from that collection.

About the Translator

Walton C. Lee, born in Taipei, Taiwan (the democratic China), is very fond of Chinese history and literature. A naturalized American citizen, he is a graduate of San Francisco State University. His goal is to introduce sophisticated Chinese culture to Western readers. Mr. Lee lives in El Cerrito, California.

Visit Walton Lee's Web site at:
http://www.geocities.com/SiliconValley/6426 and sample a few stories online!